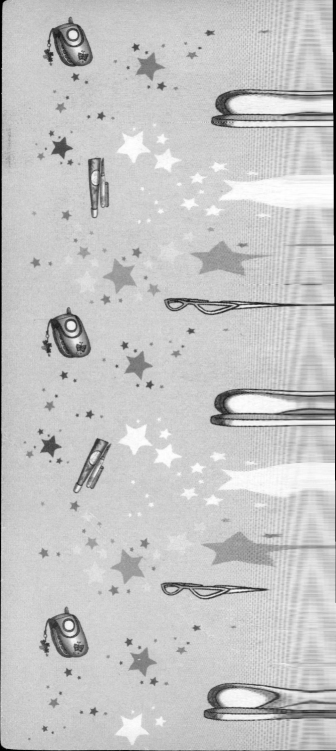

Hollie

Annabelle Starr

EGMONT

Special thanks to:

Sarah Delmege, St John's Walworth Church of England
School and Belmont Primary School

EGMONT

We bring stories to life

Published in Great Britain 2007
by Egmont UK Limited
239 Kensington High Street, London W8 6SA

Text & illustrations © 2007 Egmont UK Ltd
Text by Sarah Delmege
Illustrations by Helen Turner

ISBN 978 1 4052 3249 4

3 5 7 9 10 8 6 4 2

A CIP catalogue record for this title is available
from the British Library

Typeset by Avon DataSet Ltd, Bidford on Avon, Warwickshire
Printed and bound in Great Britain by the CPI Group

Meet the
Megastar Mysteries Team!

Hi, this is me, **Rosie Parker** (otherwise known as Nosy Parker), and these are my best mates . . .

. . . **Soph** (Sophie) **McCoy** – she's a real fashionista sista – and . . .

. . . **Abs** (Abigail) **Flynn**, who's officially une grande genius.

Here's my mum, **Liz Parker**.
Much to my embarrassment,
her fashion and music taste
is well and truly stuck in the
1980s (but despite all that
I still love her dearly) . . .

. . . and my nan,
Pam Parker, the murder-
mystery freak I mentioned
on the cover. Sometimes,
just sometimes, her crackpot
ideas do come in handy.

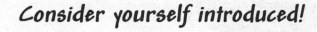

Consider yourself introduced!

Rosie's Mini Megastar Phrasebook

Want to speak our lingo, but don't know your soeurs from your signorinas? No problemo! Just use my comprehensive guide . . .

-a-rama	add this ending to a word to indicate a large quantity: e.g. 'The after-show party was celeb-a-rama'
amigo	Spanish for 'friend'
au contraire, mon frère	French for 'on the contrary, my brother'
au revoir	French for 'goodbye'
barf/barfy/barfissimo	sick/sick-making/very sick-making indeed
bien sûr, ma soeur	French for 'of course, my sister'
bon	French for 'good'
bonjour	French for 'hello'
celeb	short for 'celebrity'
convo	short for 'conversation'
cringe-fest	a highly embarrassing situation
Cringeville	a place we all visit from time to time when something truly embarrassing happens to us
cringeworthy	an embarrassing person, place or thing might be described as this
daggy	Australian for 'unfashionable' or unstylish'
doco	short for 'documentary'
exactamundo	not a real foreign word, but a great way to express your agreement with someone
exactement	French for 'exactly'

excusez moi	French for 'excuse me'
fashionista	'a keen follower of fashion' – can be teamed with 'sista' for added rhyming fun
glam	short for 'glamorous'
gorge/gorgey	short for 'gorgeous': e.g. 'the lead singer of that band is gorge/gorgey'
hilarioso	not a foreign word at all, just a great way to liven up 'hilarious'
hola, señora	Spanish for 'hello, missus'
hottie	no, this is *not* short for hot water bottle – it's how you might describe an attractive-looking boy to your friends
-issimo	try adding this ending to English adjectives for extra emphasis: e.g. coolissimo, crazissimo – très funissimo, non?
je ne sais pas	French for 'I don't know'
je voudrais un beau garçon, s'il vous plaît	French for 'I would like an attractive boy, please'
journos	short for 'journalists'
les Français	French for, erm, 'the French'
Loserville	this is where losers live, particularly evil school bully Amanda Hawkins
mais	French for 'but'
marvelloso	not technically a foreign word, just a more exotic version of 'marvellous'
massivo	Italian for 'massive'
mon amie/mes amis	French for 'my friend'/'my friends'
muchos	Spanish for 'many'

non	French for 'no'
nous avons deux garçons ici	French for 'we have two boys here'
no way, José!	'that's never going to happen!'
oui	French for 'yes'
quelle horreur!	French for 'what horror!'
quelle surprise!	French for 'what a surprise!'
sacré bleu	French for 'gosh' or even 'blimey'
stupido	this is the Italian for 'stupid' – stupid!
-tastic	add this ending to any word to indicate a lot of something: e.g. 'Abs is braintastic'
très	French for 'very'
swoonsome	decidedly attractive
si, si, signor/signorina	Italian for 'yes, yes, mister/miss'
terriblement	French for 'terribly'
une grande	French for 'a big' – add the word 'genius' and you have the perfect description of Abs
Vogue	it's only the world's most influential fashion magazine, darling!
voilà	French for 'there it is'
what's the story, Rory?	'what's going on?'
what's the plan, Stan?	'which course of action do you think we should take?'
what the crusty old grandads?	'what on earth?'
zut alors!	French for 'darn it!'

Hi Megastar reader!

My name's Annabelle Starr*. I'm a fashion stylist – just like Soph's Aunt Penny – which means it's my job to help celebrities look their best at all times.

Over the years, I've worked with all sorts of big names, some of whom also have seriously big egos! Take the time I flew all the way to Japan to style a shoot for a girl band. One of the members refused to wear the designer number I'd picked out for her and insisted on sporting a dress her mum had run up from some revolting old curtains instead. The only way I could get her to take it off was to persuade her it didn't match her pet Pekinese's outfit!

Anyway, when I first started out, I never dreamt I'd write a series of books based around my crazy celebrity experiences, but that's just what I've done with Megastar Mysteries. Rosie, Soph and Abs have just the sort of adventures I wish my friends and I could have got up to when we were teenagers!

I really hope you enjoy reading the books as much as I enjoyed writing them!

Love **Annabelle**

* I'll let you in to a little secret: this isn't my real name, but in this business you can never be too careful!

Chapter One

Argh! Double maths was *so* not my idea of fun. I closed my eyes, hoping that if I wished hard enough, the numbers in my exercise book might somehow magically arrange themselves into the answer. But when I opened my eyes, the numbers were all still there, in exactly the same order, making as little sense as ever.

I sighed heavily and stared out of the window. Maths is so annoying! I mean, seriously, when did really important stars like Madonna or the queen ever need maths in real life? The queen doesn't even carry money, for heaven's sake. Mind you, Madonna's so smart, she could probably do multiple fractions while standing on her head. I bet she could explain it to me, probably by writing a totally cool pop song about it. Imagine having Madonna as your maths teacher – coolissimo! Wouldn't that be totally great? I mean, we'd probably really hit it off. Oooh, and then she'd hear me humming to myself in class one day and realise that I was actually a really amazing singer. And she'd write me a hit record and invite me to stay in her mansion. We'd become, like, totally good friends, and some magazine like *Star Secrets* would do a feature on best friends and we'd be in it. And . . .

'Earth calling Rosie. Come in, Rosie!'

With a jolt, the happy pictures of me laughing with Madonna vanished from my head, and my brain snapped into focus. Mr Adams, my maths teacher and form tutor, was frowning at me from the front of the class.

'I'm sorry, Mr Adams,' I said, sheepishly.

'No. I'm sorry, Rosie. I'm sorry if my lesson is getting in the way of your daydream,' he said. 'I'd hate to think I was boring you.'

Uh-oh. Sarcasm. 'Sorry, Mr Adams,' I said again.

I was, too. Honestly, I really like Mr Adams. As teachers go, he's pretty cool. And he's totally good-looking too – well, for someone who's ancient. After all, he must be at least in his mid-thirties. He's got really messy dark hair and these soulful, brown eyes. And he dresses OK – even Soph thinks he's got a nice line in shirts and, believe me, that's really saying something. Mr Adams is quite funny, too – when he's not making totally teachery comments. I can't help but think he'd make a pretty good boyfriend for Mum. I mean, he obviously doesn't mind a bit of eighties music, which is a must with her. I know this because I walked into our form room the other day and he was singing a song I recognised at the top of his lungs. It was by Wham! – an eighties band and one of Mum's favourite groups, like, ever. He went so red when he saw me he could have doubled as a postbox. I really think they'd be perfect together – much better than the last guy Mum went out with, Unfunny Brian. Plus, it would be just like what happens with Mia's mum in *The Princess Diaries*, which is my favourite book. Although, obviously, there would be a few differences – like, er, me not being American. Or, um, not being a princess for that matter. But hey, you get the picture.

'Rosie Parker! I won't tell you again,' said Mr Adams. 'If you don't stop staring out of the window, you can stay behind after school.'

Honestly, do teachers learn to say these things when they're at teacher-training college? Seriously, you'd think they'd come up with something more original.

Top ten things teachers always say:

1. Would you like to share that with the rest of the class?
2. I won't tell you again, it's not clever and it's

definitely not funny!

3. Would you do that at home?
4. I've got eyes in the back of my head, you know!
5. Rosie Parker! If I'd wanted your opinion, I'd have asked for it!
6. Perhaps you'd like to take the lesson instead?
7. Would you like to spend lunchtime in the headmistress's office?
8. I'd like you to have a good, hard think about what you've done!
9. If Soph/Abs told you to jump under a bus, would you do it?
10. I think you'll find the bell is for me, not for you!

'Rosie Parker! I won't tell you again!'

See what I mean?

After that, it was a quite a relief to get to English and catch up with Soph and Abs, who are both in the same class as me. I don't want to blow my own trumpet or anything, but I'm really quite good at English. Mrs Oldham says I'm one of the best in the class. Which is handy, really, cos I want to be a writer. And who ever heard of a writer who wasn't good at English? Well, unless they were Spanish or French writers or something – and I'm guessing they'd be brilliant at Spanish or French.

'Right, class,' said Mrs Oldham, brushing down her denim skirt. 'I have some exciting news.'

I rolled my eyes and looked over at Soph, who was sitting next to me. The last time Mrs Oldham told us she had exciting news it turned out a new bookcase was being added to the library. Not exactly earth-shattering! Soph feels the same way about English as I feel about maths. She was still bent over her exercise book, scribbling frantically. At first glance, it seemed like she was trying to get her head round *Macbeth*. But I could so tell she wasn't. I leant over to have a closer look at what she was writing. Ha, I was right! She was planning her outfit for the weekend. I could see she had written the headings:

Possible outfits for wearing while shopping in town:

> Day in town (sunny)
> Day in town (cloudy)
> Day in town (rainy)

That's Soph for you – totally and utterly obsessed with clothes. I nudged her and nodded towards Mrs Oldham, who was still talking. Soph sat up immediately. Believe me, you don't want to get on the wrong side of Mrs O – she's so short-tempered, she makes Scrooge look positively chirpy.

'I'm very happy to tell you all,' Mrs Oldham said, 'that Hollie Fraser will be coming to Whitney High in a week's time to do a writing workshop.'

I gaped at her. 'Hollie Fraser?' I asked. '*The* Hollie Fraser – the one who writes the *Dirty Tricks* series?'

'Yes, Rosie,' Mrs Oldham grinned. 'The very same.'

I heard Abs squeal behind me. 'But she's amazing!' she practically shouted. 'I've read all her books – all forty-nine of them!'

Hollie Fraser is H.U.G.E.! Her first book in the *Dirty Tricks* series was the biggest-selling children's book ever. Her writing's totally amazing. She's exactly the kind of writer I want to be when I'm older. I mean, she's so good that some of her books have even been made into TV series and films. And Hollie's as famous as her books. She has loads of celebrity friends and is always at celeb-filled parties. She's even been on the cover of *Star Secrets* – the only author they've ever had as a cover star. No surprise, really, since the *Dirty Tricks* series of books had been turned into mega-successful movies that made tons of money. And now she was coming to Whitney High!

'I'm sure Ms Fraser will be delighted to hear of your enthusiasm,' said Mrs Oldham.

The bell rang just then. We all gathered up our stuff and headed for the door. Me, Abs and Soph gawped at each other once we got into the corridor, totally thrilled. We had a big hug and sort of danced around till Soph realised she was still holding her pen and I now had biro all over my shirt.

'Oh, no,' gasped Soph, catching sight of her watch. 'We're late for drama rehearsal. Time Lord's going to kill us!'

The three of us hurtled along the corridor to the assembly hall where the drama rehearsals were being held. Whitney High was taking part in a regional drama competition in a few weeks and Mr Lord was treating it as seriously as if we were up for the Oscars or something. So it wasn't surprising that he was, like, really unimpressed by our lateness.

'What time do you call this, young ladies?' he snapped as we burst through the hall door. 'I hope you have a good excuse.'

'Sorry, Mr Lord,' Abs said. 'But we just found out that Hollie Fraser is coming to do a workshop with us next week! We got a bit over-excited and lost track of time!'

Mr Lord rolled his eyes heavenward. 'I will never understand why the youth of today are so obsessed with celebrity. I used to mix with the crème de la crème of fame when I was a Cyberman in the original *Doctor Who* and you never saw me getting my knickers in a twist about it.'

I heard Soph behind me try to disguise a snigger at the idea of Time Lord wearing knickers. Fortunately, he was too busy telling us off to notice. 'You know, I just don't get what's so great about Hollie Fraser anyway. She's not that good a writer. Now, my writing really could have set the world on fire. I had brilliant ideas for books, plays and even a TV series that I still believe could have been as big as *Doctor Who*, but I felt that mine was a different calling. Hard as it was to deprive the world of my talent, I felt it was more important to help shape the stars of the future, like Amanda over there.'

I stared over at Amanda Hawkins' smug, mocking face. *Yeah, right, if Amanda Hawkins is the star of the future then I'm Justin Timberlake's new girlfriend*. Behind me, Soph started making gagging noises.

'Yes, Miss McCoy?' said Time Lord. 'Do you have something to say?'

'Er, no,' Soph smiled, innocently. 'I just felt really sick for a moment.'

Time Lord narrowed his eyes at her, then shook his head. 'Right, well, may I suggest that you three make sure you are on time from now on. We have a regional drama competition to win!'

GREAT. JUST GREAT!

Chapter Two

I still couldn't believe it! Hollie Fraser was coming to
our school! I mean, of course, I *believed* it. Mrs
Oldham was hardly likely to lie about it. That would
land her in real trouble with Meanie Greenie, our
head teacher. But just occasionally, when I wasn't
concentrating, my mind would suddenly yell, *What?*
Hollie Fraser *at* Whitney High?

In fact, it was doing that right now. Although
that could have had something to do with the fact
that I was round at Soph's with Abs, watching all
the *Dirty Tricks* movies.

'Josh Stevens is totally gorgeous!' Soph sighed, as the camera moved in to a close-up of his chocolate-brown eyes.

'I know!' I agreed. 'Hollie is so lucky to go out with him.'

'Yeah,' said Abs. 'But he's lucky too. After all, she picked him from thousands of other wannabe actors to be in her film.'

That was another fabtastic thing about Hollie Fraser. When the auditions had been held for *Dirty Tricks*, she had insisted that no big names should be used for the main parts in the first movie. (Although loads of celebs had featured in the movies as well – there was even a rumour that superstar singer Mirage Mullins would be appearing in the next one.) I read in an interview that Josh Stevens had always dreamt of being a star, and when he read about the auditions, he took a sickie from his day job as a postman and turned up to audition for the part of Mark Green. When he saw the thousands of other hopefuls that had turned up, he didn't think he stood a chance.

But when he walked into the audition room, Hollie jumped up with excitement. And not just because he was jaw-droppingly gorgeous. Apparently, Hollie knew he would be perfect for the role of Mark Green from the minute she laid eyes on him. Hollie had also said in many an interview that she'd based the character on her ideal boyfriend – so it was no wonder that the two had fallen head-over-heels in love during filming. I mean, it must have been like seeing your Mr Right leaping straight off the page.

'Oooh,' gasped Soph, hugging a cushion. 'Do you think Josh might come with Hollie to school tomorrow? I mean, how, amazing would that be?'

'Wow!' I breathed out a mouthful of salt-and-vinegar crisps, 'Just imagine being that close to Mark Green!'

There was a short silence. I looked up to see Abs and Soph grinning at me.

'What?' I said.

'Please don't embarrass us by calling him Mark to his face.' Abs smirked at me.

'You know what I mean,' I said, feeling my face flush hotter than a spicy curry. 'And you promised we weren't going to talk about it any more.'

So, there was this tiny little incident when I was doing work experience at *Star Secrets* magazine a few months ago. We were behind the scenes on the set of my favourite soap, *Honeydale*, and I accidentally kept calling all the stars by their screen names. I mean, it was a tiny little mistake. It could have happened to anyone. Really – it could.

Abs leant back on the sofa, chewing a fingernail thoughtfully. 'I can't believe that the next book is the last in the *Dirty Tricks* series,' she said.

'Do you reckon Hollie might give away some clues tomorrow?' asked Soph. 'I mean, how cool would it be if we knew what was going to happen before the rest of the world found out?'

'I doubt she'll tell us anything,' said Abs. 'But she has said one of the major characters will die at the end.'

'Apparently, Hollie's last chapter is hidden in a

safe in her house,' I chipped in. 'She wrote it before she even started the first chapter of the first book! It's like, the biggest, topissimo secret. No one apart from Hollie knows – not even Mark. I mean, Josh. And if anyone did manage to get hold of it, it'd be worth hundreds of thousands of pounds.'

'Wow!' breathed Soph. 'Just imagine how many clothes you could buy with all that money! Anyway, come and help me choose which accessories to wear tomorrow – I have to look my fashionista best to meet a world-famous author!'

* * *

The next day the three of us met at the end of Whitney Road to walk to school together.

'Abs,' I exclaimed, as she came into view, totally out of breath, 'what the crusty old grandads have you got in your bag? It's almost as big as you are.'

'I know!' she puffed, heaving it off her shoulders and letting it drop on to the pavement next to us. I swear, I almost felt the ground shudder at the weight of it. 'I've got all of Hollie Fraser's books for her to sign.'

'All of them?' I asked.

Abs nodded.

'All forty-nine of them?!' I checked incredulously.

'Yes!' said Abs.

I stared at her. This was totally un-Abs-like behaviour. I mean, she's the sensible one out of the three of us. Her brain is huge – seriously, it's like the size of a planet. And a big planet at that. I watched in amazement as she picked the bag back up off the pavement and heaved it back on to her shoulders, almost toppling over backwards from the sheer weight of it.

I looked at Soph to see what she was making of this, but she was no longer listening. She was staring over my shoulder, her mouth gaping open so wide she could seriously be mistaken for a letterbox.

'Soph?' I said.

'Look at that!' she whispered. I turned and

blinked in disbelief. Word had obviously got out that Hollie Fraser was visiting Whitney High today. The road was jam-packed with cars. There were photographers and local-news film crews everywhere. Amanda Hawkins and her two cronies – Lara Neils and Keira Roberts – were preening for the cameras. Amanda was flicking her hair so much, she was in danger of taking a photographer's eye out.

'Like anyone would want to see their ugly faces on TV,' Soph hissed. 'It would seriously put the whole of the country off their breakfast!'

Suddenly a sleek, black car appeared and pulled up to the kerb. The door opened and Hollie Fraser stepped out gracefully. There was a pause for a moment, then the photographers surged forward, shouting, 'Hollie!' 'Hollie!' 'Over here! Hollie!'

'This is so exciting!' Soph shouted.

The three of us watched as Hollie stopped, smiling and waving for the cameras. The news crews gathered around her.

'I just want to say it's a complete pleasure to

come to a school like Whitney High,' she said. 'After all, it's the children who read my books who have made me so famous and it's a privilege to spend time with some of them. And if I can inspire any children to write by doing workshops like this, then I'll really feel like I've achieved something.'

Mrs Oldham pushed her way through the crowd, dressed in her best checked shirt and a crisply ironed denim skirt.

'It's a pleasure to meet you, Ms Fraser,' she said, frowning at the photographers.

'Please call me Hollie.' The author smiled at her. 'Ms Fraser sounds so formal.'

'If you'd like to come this way, Ms – er, I mean Hollie, I'll show you to the assembly hall where we'll be having the writing workshop.'

'Check out her shoes,' gasped Soph. 'They're Fabconis!'

'I know!' I said. 'She buys herself a pair every time she has a book published. It's her gift to herself.'

'Come on!' said Soph, brandishing her mobile phone. 'I *have* to get a photo of them. They'd make a brilliant screensaver. And,' she added sadly, 'it'll probably be the nearest I get to a pair – no matter how many Saturdays I work at Dream Beauty salon.'

Grabbing me and Abs by the arm, she pulled us through the school gates.

'Out of my way, girls!' came a voice. 'OUT OF MY WAY!'

Startled, we stepped aside as Time Lord came rushing past. His long coat and trainers were practically a blur as he hurried past. In his rush, he accidentally bumped into Abs, causing her to topple over backwards and end up flat on her back. She was totally weighed down by the books in her bag, waving her arms and her legs ineffectually like an upside-down tortoise.

Time Lord rushed on, oblivious to the chaos he had left behind him.

'Ms Fraser! Coo-ee! Ms Fraser!' he shouted, charging towards a slightly scared-looking Hollie, and pumping her hand up and down like his life depended on it.

'It's . . . a . . . pleasure . . . to . . . meet . . . you!' he gasped, completely out of breath and over-excited. 'I'm a fellow-writer and actor. You might have seen me in *Doctor Who.*'

'Really?' said Hollie. 'I love that show. Are you in it at the moment?'

'Well, no,' said Time Lord, flushing bright red. 'It was an earlier series. I was a Cyberman.'

'Oh,' said Hollie. 'Well, um, that's great. Well done you. Have you done anything since?'

'Well, no,' said Time Lord, flushing even brighter red. 'I decided to put my career on hold to work with future talent. But I think the world is ready to receive my talent again.'

'Right,' said Hollie. 'Um . . .'

'I'd love to talk to you – artist to artist. I have my show-reel here and my latest screenplay for you to read.' Time Lord shoved a CD and a huge sheaf of paper into a very surprised-looking Hollie's arms. He gripped her arm. 'And I can't help but think I'd be perfect in one of your films. Perhaps you could write a part for me?'

HONESTLY, THAT MAN IS SUCH A BIG FAT FAKE. HE BANGS ON ENDLESSLY AT US ABOUT HOW CELEBRITIES ARE NOTHING SPECIAL AND WE SHOULDN'T BE IMPRESSED BY THEM. THEN HE PRACTICALLY HAS A FIT HIMSELF WHEN HE COMES INTO CONTACT WITH ONE!

'Mr Lord!' barked Mrs Oldham. 'Get a grip on yourself, man – this is neither the time nor the place. Leave our guest alone. I will see you in the staffroom later.' She turned to Hollie. 'I can only apologise, Ms Fraser. We expect this kind of behaviour from our pupils, not from our staff.' She glared at Time Lord. If looks could kill, he'd have been toast.

Me and Soph looked at each other and cracked up, holding on to one another for support. I was laughing so hard, I honestly thought I might throw up.

'When you two have finished,' Abs grumbled from the floor where she was still lying, trapped by her bag of books, 'I'd quite like some help getting up.'

Chapter Three

Having got Abs back on to her feet, we rushed into the assembly hall for the writing workshop. The room was packed, with everyone chatting excitedly. News of Time Lord's attempt to be discovered by Hollie Fraser had spread, and the school grapevine had gone into mega-drive.

'I heard he was begging her to cast him in her next movie,' Becky Blakeney from my geography class was whispering as me, Abs and Soph squeezed into some spare seats.

'Yeah,' added Frankie Gabriel, 'apparently he

was holding on to Hollie Fraser by her ankle and Mrs Oldham had to drag him off.'

I grinned at Abs and Soph. No way was Time Lord going to live this down any time soon.

Mrs Oldham walked on to the stage, followed by a subdued-looking Time Lord.

'Good morning, everyone,' she said. 'Our special guest today needs no introduction, so please welcome Ms Hollie Fraser.'

As Hollie walked out on to the stage, the whole assembly hall went crazy. People were standing on their chairs, whistling and shouting. Hollie held up her hands and grinned at all of us, waiting for the noise to quieten down.

'Wow!' she said. 'What a welcome. I feel like a rock star! Helloooooo Whitney High!'

We all cheered in response. She laughed and winked at us. 'Sorry, I couldn't help myself!'

We listened, totally enthralled, as Hollie told us what it's like to be an author. It was so interesting, especially when she said she still wrote her books in a notebook with a pen, and only typed them up when she was finished. She told us all about how she started to write, and her early days when she wrote articles and short stories for magazines.

'Oooh, it's just like you.' Soph nudged me. 'Just think, you could be the next Hollie Fraser!'

'Sophie McCoy!' barked Mrs Oldham. 'Stop talking!'

Soph blushed bright red. Hollie carried on talking. 'Then, one day, I got a call from a book publisher who'd seen some of my stories. They asked if I was interested in writing a series of books for them. Of course, I jumped at the chance. And that was when I realised how much I loved writing books – the ideas just kept coming, and –'

'Oh, I know what you mean, Hollie,' interrupted Time Lord. 'We writers just can't stop those ideas flowing. Why, only the other day I had this brilliant idea –'

'Mr Lord,' said Mrs Oldham, warningly. 'Much as we're all interested in your ideas, perhaps you could let Ms Fraser continue.'

'Oh, yes, right,' said Mr Lord. 'Do carry on, Hollie. I'll tell you more about my ideas later.'

'Right, um, thanks,' said Hollie. 'Well, as I was saying, I was lucky enough to find a publisher who really believed in me and my ideas. I always thought that it would be amazing if a few children loved my stories. But I never for one minute expected that they'd be so successful, or thought that they'd be made into films. When I got the phone call to say a film company was interested, I honestly thought someone was pulling my leg.' She paused and smiled round the hall at us all. 'But I don't want to talk at you all morning. How about you ask me some questions and I'll do my best to answer?'

My hand shot into the air, along with practically every other hand in the rest of the room. I tapped my foot impatiently as Hollie answered question after boring question. Especially when Time Lord kept interrupting to talk about films and his 'fellow actors' – like they were in the same league. I could feel Soph's shoulders shaking with silent laughter next to me.

Finally it was my turn. Hollie smiled at me. 'Yes?'

'What's it like going out with Josh Stevens?' I asked.

Hollie looked flustered. 'Well – it's, um – well, it's fine.'

Fine? *Fine??!!* I wanted to shout. This was Josh Stevens – the most gorgeous specimen to hit the big screen since, like, ever! *Are you crazy?*

'Yes, he is gorgeous. And no, I'm not crazy . . .' smiled Hollie. Oh, sacré bleu, had I said that last bit aloud? I glanced at Abs and Soph. By the shocked looks on their faces, I had.

OOPS!

'I'm afraid it's just not something I like to talk about.' She smiled apologetically. I frowned. I had read loads of interviews where Hollie had been only too happy to talk about Josh. What had changed? Maybe everything wasn't what it seemed? Although how anything could possibly be wrong when you were dating someone as seriously gorgeous as Josh Stevens, I had no idea. I raised an eyebrow at Soph and Abs. I could feel my mystery radar totally kicking into gear.

'Right,' said Mrs Oldham. 'I think you'll all agree, this has been a fascinating morning. Now we'll take a quick break, then Hollie will be setting you all a writing task. I hope you'll all join me in giving Ms Fraser a huge round of applause to thank her for her time.'

Me, Abs and Soph rushed to the front of the hall to get Hollie's autograph. She happily signed my English book and even let Soph take a picture of her Fabconis. Her smile faltered somewhat when Abs produced her bag of forty-nine books but, like a true professional, she picked up a pen and started signing.

'If you don't mind, I'll finish these later,' she said after doing the tenth one. Good thing too, because the others who were waiting in the queue were starting to get dead stroppy.

'She's so cool,' grinned Abs as we made our way to the canteen to grab a drink.

'Totally,' said Soph. She got out her phone and stared at her photo of Hollie's Fabconis for, like, the trillionth time. 'What I wouldn't give for her shoe collection.'

'Hmm,' I said. 'But did you see how funny she got when I asked her about Josh? Something's definitely going on there.'

Soph shook her head. 'Maybe she was just shy,' she said. 'I mean, I don't know about you, but I wouldn't want to discuss my love life in front of a room full of giggling fourteen-year-olds.'

'What love life?' said Abs. 'I don't think kissing your poster of Josh Stevens every night before you go to sleep counts.' She turned her back on us and started running her hands up and down her back, making it look as if they were someone else's hands, wiggling her bum and making kissing noises. 'You love him, you want to kiss him, you want to marry him, you . . .'

'Shut up!' said Soph.

'No, you shut up!' said Abs.

'You.'

'You.'

'No. You.'

I rolled my eyes. I didn't care what they said, there was definitely some reason why Hollie didn't want to talk about Josh, and I was determined to find out what it was.

* * *

The rest of the writing workshop was totally coolissimo. Hollie told us to write a short story. It could be about anything we wanted, but it had to involve an animal and something sad. I stared round the room, waiting for inspiration to strike. Next to me, Soph was scribbling away happily. Two minutes later, she put her hand in the air.

'Yes, Sophie?' said Mrs Oldham.

'I've finished.' Soph grinned.

Mrs O stared at her in amazement and walked over to read what she'd written. '"One day I found a dog. I asked my mum if we could keep him. She said no. I was sad. The end."' Mrs O's forehead went all wrinkly. 'Um, I don't think this is really what Ms Fraser is looking for.'

'Why not?' said Soph. 'It's about an animal and something sad happens.'

Mrs Oldham sighed heavily. 'OK, Sophie. You can go.' She looked around the room. 'When you've finished, give your story in to me and leave the room QUIETLY. Other people are still working.'

Soph winked at me, picked up her stuff and practically skipped out of the room. Have I mentioned she really doesn't like English?

Pushing my hair back, I started to write about a girl who finds a stray rabbit and takes it home and looks after it. But one day the rabbit escapes from its hutch and gets run over. The girl finds it in the street, still alive, but only just. She rushes to the vet who operates on it, but it's touch and go whether the rabbit will actually pull through. It was totally sad. Even I was nearly crying, and it was my own story!

'Rosie?' I looked up. Mrs Oldham was smiling at me. 'Why don't you finish that tomorrow? Everyone else handed theirs in ages ago.'

I looked around the room – it was empty. I'd been so absorbed, I hadn't noticed everyone else leaving! I stood up and started packing away my things. I glanced over at Hollie. She was still making her way through Abs's mountain of books, patiently signing each and every one. Sacré bleu, her arm must have been aching.

'Um, Ms Fraser?' I said. 'I'm sorry if I crossed the line by asking you about Josh.'

Hollie's hand stopped moving. She looked up at me. 'It's fine, honestly. I just prefer not to talk about my personal life. You have to keep some things private, you know?'

She smiled, but I couldn't help but notice that it didn't quite reach her eyes. And as she picked up the pen to continue working through Abs's books, I could see her hand shaking. Something was very definitely wrong, or my mum wasn't an embarrassingly huge fan of eighties music!

* * *

The next night, I was at home in my bedroom, still trying (and failing miserably) to get my head around multiple fractions. One question: why do multiple fractions even exist? Why? Why? Whhhhhhyyyyyyyyyyyyy? (OK, technically that's four questions, but you get the picture.)

Just then a message from Soph flashed up on my computer.

FashionPolice: Turn on the news NOW.
NosyParker: Why?
FashionPolice: Just DO IT, Rosie! Sacré bleu!
NosyParker: OK, OK! I'm doing it!

I picked up my remote control and turned on the TV, then gasped as I listened to the news report. Hollie Fraser had gone missing! No way! I watched, totally gobsmacked, as the story unfolded. A concerned-looking reporter stood outside Hollie's huge country home, talking into the camera.

'Police are looking into the possibility that Hollie Fraser might have been kidnapped, although no ransom note has been received yet. Rumours are rife that it might be a jealous rival trying to stop the manuscript of her latest book from being published. However, others suggest that Hollie may have cracked under the pressure of finishing her eagerly anticipated children's book. There is speculation that she may be hiding out, suffering from writer's block. Whatever lies behind it, the fact remains that for the moment, the whereabouts of Holly Fraser is a mystery. Now back to the studio.'

I rolled my eyes at the TV. If it was a simple case of writer's block then surely Hollie would have let someone know. I mean, she wouldn't just be sitting somewhere, letting all this media frenzy develop. Seriously, it hardly took a genius to work that out. I just hoped the police had more sense than that reporter. Tutting, I flicked through the channels and froze as a familiar gorgeous face filled the screen. Josh Stevens. I watched as he gave a tearful interview, begging for Hollie's safe return and saying that he would pay any ransom, no matter how big. As he spoke, he wiped tears from his eyes.

My computer beeped.

> **FashionPolice**: How CUTE does Josh look?
> **NosyParker**: Sophie McCoy! Hollie Fraser HAS JUST GONE MISSING!!
> **FashionPolice**: I know. But really, sooo cute!

Honestly, I give up!

Josh was still talking on the TV. My heart went out to him as he looked directly into the camera, his voice thickening as tears swam in those famous chocolate-brown eyes.

'I just hope she's OK. I've been so looking forward to playing Mark in the last film and I really hope it will still happen, as I just know it's going to be the best yet. Hollie's talent is amazing and I know she has brilliant things planned for my character.'

I jumped as someone snorted behind me. I spun round. Nan was standing in the doorway.

'Nan!' I grumbled. 'You almost gave me a heart attack!'

'Never trust anyone with such a pretty face,' she said, nodding wisely at the TV, where Josh was still talking. 'You know what they say – angelic face hides devilish heart.'

'Who says that?' I said. 'I've never heard anyone say any such thing.'

'Well, if they don't, they should,' said Nan. 'Chuntering on about his own career when the supposed love of his life has just gone missing.'

'Nan!' I exclaimed. 'You only have to look at him to see how heartbroken he is.'

'Hmm,' she said, not sounding convinced in the slightest. 'Anyway, there's a rerun of *Miss Marple* just starting, so I'll see you later.'

My nan is totally murder-mystery obsessed. She can practically recite every single line of every single episode of *Murder, She Wrote*. She totally thinks she's the real-life equivalent of Jessica Fletcher, the writer/amateur detective from the series. She's even started writing her own murder-mystery stories. As far as I can make out, the biggest crime that's happened so far is someone stealing all the toffees from the local old people's home.

I mean, seriously, I love my family to death, but having a mother whose mission in life is to bring eighties music to a modern audience and a murder-mystery obsessed nan can be a bit trying.

Chapter Four

With the regional competition only a couple of days away, we were spending every spare minute in drama rehearsals. I was expecting Time Lord to be in full drama mode, shouting and screaming at everyone – apart from evil Amanda Hawkins who could do no wrong in his eyes.

Take our last rehearsal, for example. He'd stopped the play halfway through to give me a hard time about my acting. I wouldn't have minded if I had a huge part. But no, I was playing the part of . . . wait for it . . . an old lady in the crowd. I was on stage for, oooh, about ten seconds. I didn't even get to speak – I just had to walk across the stage, stopping to pick a pretend flower. I'd only just walked on to the stage when Time Lord stopped me.

'Rosie Parker, you are meant to be an old lady,' he said, making a grand gesture with his hand, as if he was giving an Oscar-winning performance. 'I don't want you to just *look* old, I want you to *feel* old! I want you to feel every single wrinkle on your face, the tiredness in your bones, the failing of your sight, the hunching of your spine. Next time I see you, I expect you to look ninety-eight years old! Got it?'

'Um, yes, Mr Lord,' I'd said, slightly alarmed but prepared to try.

So today, when I bent over to pick the pretend flower and completely forgot that I was meant to be ninety-eight years old with backache, I was expecting Mr Lord to have a fit. But to my surprise, he didn't even seem to notice.

'What's up with Time Lord?' I whispered, as

I joined Soph at the back of the hall where she was busy making costumes.

'I don't know,' she whispered back. 'I showed him Amanda's costume earlier and, as he reached out to touch one of the sleeves, the hem totally unravelled! He didn't even flinch!'

We both looked up as Amanda Hawkins ended one of her scenes. There was a pause while she smiled expectantly in Time Lord's direction, waiting for his usual flood of praise and congratulations on her acting – which as far as I can make out consists of lots of fluttering eyelashes and flicking of hair. But there was nothing. Zero. Zilch. Time Lord didn't even look up from the desk where he was bent over a bit of paper, writing frantically. Her face was a picture and she flounced off the stage. Something was wrong here. What was the story?

Abs came rushing over to me and Soph. 'You guys are not going to believe this!' she said. 'I was walking past Time Lord's desk when I spotted this bit of paper on the floor.' She thrust it under our noses. Confused, I started to read:

Dirty Tricks: The final book
By Tim Lord

'No *way*!' I gasped.

'Way!' nodded Abs. 'Time Lord's only writing the ending for the *Dirty Tricks* series – just in case Hollie doesn't re-appear!'

UNBELIEVABLE!!

* * *

After drama, me, Abs and Soph headed back to my house. I was expecting it to be empty as Mum would be at work at the council offices and Nan always spends Tuesday afternoons at the library. She picks up her latest murder-mystery novel, then heads to the local café – Trotters – for a cup of tea and an iced bun. But as we walked up the drive, the door swung open and there was Mum, wearing a 'You Don't Have To Love Eighties

Music To Work Here But It Helps' T-shirt and skin-tight, animal-print leggings with neon-pink stilettos. Seriously, would it kill her to wear jeans and trainers like normal mums?

'Girls!' she cried, running over to give us all a hug. Honestly, you'd think we'd been separated for years – not one school day. 'You're just in time to watch me go through my latest routine,' she smiled excitedly, ushering us all into the kitchen.

'Shouldn't you be at work, Mum?' I asked.

'Oh, no, Mr Oldbury gave me the afternoon off,' she smiled. 'Which is handy, cos I needed to work on this new routine.'

Have I mentioned my mum's in an eighties tribute band called the Banana Splits? It's named after my mum's all-time fave girl group, Bananarama. They were as big in the eighties as Girls Aloud are now.

Grinning at us, she turned her CD player up to full volume. With closed eyes and her tongue poking out, she started going through her moves. Oh, the shame. I couldn't bring myself to look at

Soph and Abs. Your mum's backside shimmying across the room encased in animal-print lycra is so not a sight you ever want your friends to see. Ever.

After about a million years, the music ended. Finally, it was over! Abs and Soph burst into applause, while I wished the ground would open up and swallow me whole.

'That was brillissimo,' said Abs.

'Totally, Mrs P,' said Soph. 'I loved it. And, if you want any help with your outfits, then let me know.'

'Well, actually,' Mum grinned delightedly, 'I do have a pair of shiny gold trousers . . .'

I groaned and closed my eyes.

'. . . that the zip is broken on. I was going to take them to get mended but if you don't mind . . .'

'My pleasure, Mrs P,' said Soph.

Mum hurried off to fetch the trousers. I rolled my eyes. I just hoped that Mum would dress a bit more – well – *normally* for the regional drama competition. Especially if Mr Adams was ever going to notice her and, you know, ask her out.

Just then the front door opened and Nan came bustling in. 'Well,' she said, 'You'll never guess who I just bumped into in Trotters!'

'Um . . .' I grinned at Abs and Soph. 'James Bond? The queen? No, I've got it – Angela Lansbury!'

Nan gave me a piercing look. 'Hollie Fraser.'

'*What?*' gasped Abs and Soph.

'Yeah, right,' I said. 'If you saw Hollie Fraser, then I'm a fried egg.'

'That's enough of your cheek, Rosie Parker,' said Nan. 'As I was saying, it was definitely Hollie Fraser. I even had a nice chat with her – such a wonderfully polite manner.' She paused and looked pointedly at me. 'She was wearing a lovely headscarf, and I said to her that it would make a beautiful present for my friend Marilyn. She was ever so helpful, she gave me the make and everything. I wrote it down.' She rummaged in her bag, pulled out a notebook and flicked through the pages. 'Oh, yes, Beth Ridiston.'

'*Beth Ridiston?*' said Soph. 'But she's a really

expensive, exclusive designer! I saw some of her stuff in *Vogue* last month.'

'Oh, I don't think so, dear,' said Nan. 'Between you and me, I don't think Hollie has much money. Mrs Trotter told me that she'd been coming in every lunchtime and orders one cup of coffee, one tap water and always goes for the cheapest food on the menu. Plus, when it comes to paying, she always counts out loose change.'

'Well, that settles it, then,' I said. 'It definitely wasn't Hollie. She's hardly strapped for cash. She's one of the richest people in the country! You've been watching too many murder mysteries, Nan.'

'You can mock, young lady,' said Nan. 'But there's nothing wrong with my eyes. It was definitely Hollie Fraser.'

'Whatever you say, Nan,' I sighed, looking at Abs and Soph in exasperation. 'Whatever you say.'

Honestly, it's like living in a madhouse!

* * *

The next evening, I was meant to be doing my English homework, but was actually instant-messaging Abs, when Soph's screen name flashed up:

FashionPolice: YOU ARE SOOO NOT GOING TO BELIEVE THIS!

SweetiePie: What? And stop shouting.

FashionPolice: sorry, but this is UNBELIEVABLE!!!!!

NosyParker: What is?!

FashionPolice: Well, I was putting a new zip into your mum's trousers, Rosie, when I accidentally ripped them.

NosyParker: Fantastissimo. They. Are. Hideous.

FashionPolice: Well, actually they're very fashion-forward. They're total clubbing-girl-around-town-too-cool-to-care.

NosyParker: Soph! My mum's in her thirties. She's not cool, and even if she doesn't care that she's being seen out in public wearing skin-tight gold trousers, I do!

SweetiePie: Can we get to the point, please? I'm getting older here.

FashionPolice: So I headed to the charity shop round the corner from my house. And luckily they had a really similar pair of trousers.

NosyParker: Noooooooooooo!

FashionPolice: I'm ignoring that. Anyway, when I came out, I passed Belle's Boutique. You know, that really expensive designer re-sale shop where people sell off last season's designer clothes. Oooh, la, la! I wish I could afford to shop there!

SweetiePie: Soph, is this story actually going anywhere?

FashionPolice: Sorry. But it's worth the wait. Honestly. Right, so as I was saying – the Fabconi shoes that Hollie was wearing when she came in to school were in the window! Your nan's right, Rosie, she's in Borehurst!!!

SweetiePie: Soph, much as I hate to break it to you, there's more than one pair of red Fabconis in the world. It doesn't mean that they're Hollie's.

NosyParker: Abs is right. It's just a coincidence.

FashionPolice: I knew you'd say that. So I've sent you both proof.

Just then, my phone beeped. I picked it up. Two photo messages from Soph had come through. I opened up the first one. It was the pic of Hollie's shoes that Soph took on the day of the writing workshop and has been using as a screensaver. There was a message attached to it from Soph:

Check out the white paint on the heel!

Sure enough, I could make out a faint strip of

paint on the heel, as if Hollie had stood too close to some wet paint while wearing them. I opened the next message. It was a picture of the shoes in the window of Belle's Boutique. There was another message from Soph:

Look at the heel!

I peered closely at the photo. No way! There was the same strip of paint; it was the same pair of shoes! That only meant one thing! I rushed back to my computer and started typing:

NosyParker: No way, José! Hollie Fraser IS in Borehurst! Or at the very least, her shoes are! We've got to find her!

Chapter Five

The next morning, before school started, the three of us met on Whitney Road.

'What's the plan, Stan?' asked Soph.

'I think we should head to Trotters at lunchtime,' said Abs. 'After all, that's where your nan reckoned she saw Hollie, and didn't Mrs Trotter say she'd been in there every day? We can easily get there and make it back in plenty of time for afternoon lessons.'

'But, what the crusty old grandads is she doing in Boringhurst?' I said. 'She must know there's a nationwide search going on for her. It doesn't make any sense.'

'Well, there's only one way to find out,' said Abs, as we walked through the school gates. 'I'll see you both here at lunchtime.'

* * *

I knew I wasn't going to be able to concentrate all morning. Luckily, it wasn't too demanding. I had a spare period, followed by PE. Well, I thought it was lucky, until Amanda Witchface Hawkins took advantage of me obviously paying no attention and bounced a netball right off my head. On purpose.

'Ouch!' I shrieked.

'Oh, I'm sorry,' said Amanda, 'Did the nasty ball hit your poor little head? Diddums!' She raised her eyebrows innocently and Lara Neils gave a snort of laughter.

I stared at them in disgust. Well, she'd be laughing on the other side of her smug, mocking face when me, Abs and Soph solved the mystery of the disappearance of Hollie Fraser. Oooh, I could just imagine the press conference now. The journalists would ask us loads of questions about what had happened. They would be amazed to find out that I wanted to be a writer and had articles published in *Star Secrets* magazine. And a publisher would read all about it in a newspaper and would ring me and ask me to write a book about my experiences. And I'd make sure I wrote about every single time Amanda Hawkins and her cronies made Soph's, Abs's and my lives a misery. And the whole world would realise what a horrible, nasty piece of work she was. And she'd be shunned by everyone; old ladies would hit her over the head with their umbrellas in the street and . . .

'Rosie Parker!'

My mind snapped back to the present. Miss Osbourne, my PE teacher, was standing with her hands on her hips, frowning at me. She looked seriously unimpressed.

'As you're obviously too busy daydreaming to pay any attention to the game, perhaps a few laps around the field will help you to concentrate.'

GREAT. JUST GREAT.

✳ ✳ ✳

'Nice look!' said Soph as I puffed up next to them by the school gates. I was red-faced, sweaty and still in my tracksuit; I didn't have time to get changed or have a shower if we were to make it into town and back before afternoon registration.

'I know, I know,' I said. 'Come on, let's go or we'll never make it back in time.'

Ten minutes later, we were standing outside Trotters.

'You know,' said Abs, 'I still think we've got it wrong. I can't believe Hollie Fraser would just be sitting calmly in a café, drinking coffee, when there's a nationwide hunt going on for her! I mean, she seemed so normal and down-to-earth when she came into school. I reckon the newspapers have got it right – she must have been kidnapped.'

'Think again,' said Soph, nodding over her shoulder. 'Hollie Fraser's sitting right there. Look!'

And there she was. She was wearing a headscarf and there was a pair of sunglasses on the table next to her. But it was definitely her, eating a cheese roll, as if she didn't have a care in the world!

'Right!' stormed Abs. 'I'm going to give her a piece of my mind. How could she just pretend to go missing, leaving poor Josh broken-hearted? I'm never reading another one of her books again – I don't care how good they are!'

Abs yanked the door open so violently, I was afraid it was going to come off its hinges. I'm not joking. She marched into the café, her brown bob bouncing. You could tell she was super-determined to have her say. Me and Soph exchanged worried glances.

'I wouldn't want to be in Hollie Fraser's shoes right now,' whispered Soph.

'I know!' I said. Abs is one of the most chilled people I know, but when she flies into one of her rages, she's so scary she's hairy. Soph waggled her eyebrows at me, then the two of us scuttled in behind Abs.

Hollie looked up as the three of us approached her table. Her face went white as she took in our Whitney High school uniforms. Well, Abs and Soph's school uniforms. I'm not sure that my tracksuit would have meant very much to her. Her eyes were darting from side to side, as if she was looking for an escape route. She pushed back her chair and started to get up, before sinking back down into her seat and shooting us such a pleading look that it even stopped Abs dead in her tracks.

'P-p-please!' she stuttered, clearly recognising us. 'Don't give me away!' She gestured at all of us to sit down.

Abs sat in the empty chair opposite Hollie, glaring at her with her arms crossed, while me and Soph grabbed chairs from neighbouring tables.

'Give us one good reason why we shouldn't tell people where you are,' Abs hissed.

Hollie covered her face with her hands. Oooh, this was quite exciting! It was a bit like being in a gangster movie. I looked from Abs to Hollie and back again. I honestly half expected them to start talking out of the side of their mouths in American accents.

'We're waiting!' snarled Abs.

'You don't understand,' said Hollie.

'Explain it to us, then,' Abs snapped. Sacré bleu, she was good!

Just then, Mrs Trotter bustled up. She'd been watching us from her stool by the till since Abs had burst into the café and was obviously trying to earwig, to find out what was going on.

'What can I get you?' she asked, her eyes roaming over us.

'Um, I thought we had to order at the till,' I said. Nan was always moaning about the lack of waitress service in Trotters.

'Well, yes, normally,' said Mrs Trotter. 'But

we're trying out waitress service today.'

'I didn't get any waitress service,' said a man at the next table.

'Neither did I!' said an old lady, at the table next to him.

'We've, er, we've only just started it,' said Mrs Trotter.

'In that case, I'll have a toasted tea cake,' said the old lady.

'Yeah, and I'll have another cup of tea,' added the man.

'And we'll have three strawberry milkshakes and three cheese toasties,' chirped Soph.

'I've only got one pair of hands!' said Mrs Trotter, looking a bit panicky. 'You'll all have to come to the till when your order's ready.'

Abs waited till she'd gone back to her stool, then looked back at Hollie.

'Well?' she said.

'OK, I'll tell you,' sighed Hollie. 'And when I've finished, I hope you'll understand why I've done this and you'll keep my secret.' She rubbed her hands across her forehead and took a deep breath, then started to explain.

'It was Josh, you see. He kept pestering and pestering me to find out what happened to Mark. And I wouldn't tell him, which drove him crazy. He kept saying if I loved him, I'd tell him. He couldn't understand that me not telling him had nothing to do with how I felt about him. It's just that my writing's so important to me, I couldn't risk anyone finding out what happened in the end. And it wasn't even just up to me. If word got out, there was so much to lose. Just think what it would mean to all the readers if they saw the ending splashed across the papers before they had a chance to read it themselves! But Josh couldn't understand. He was completely obsessed.

'Anyway, one day I got back from shopping and Josh was waiting by the door. I knew as soon as I saw his face that he'd read the ending, and I was right. He'd watched me put the manuscript away in the safe the night before and memorised the code. Then, as soon as I went out, he'd opened the safe and read the last chapter. He went crazy!'

'But why would he go crazy just because he read the last chapter?' asked Soph. 'I don't understand.'

'I do,' said Abs. She reached across the table and touched Hollie's hand. 'Mark Green dies at the end of the book, doesn't he?'

Hollie stared at her for a moment, then nodded. 'Yes,' she said softly. 'Mark dies. I'm so sorry to have given away the ending. I remember what fans you are from when I met you all at Whitney High. I hope it hasn't spoiled the series for you.'

Abs leant forward. 'It's fine,' she said. 'We understand. But tell us what happened.'

'Yes,' said Soph. 'How does he die? What happens?'

Abs glared at her meaningfully. 'I meant,' she said slowly, 'tell us what happened with Josh.'

'Sorry,' said Soph.

'He shouted at me, saying that he couldn't believe I'd killed him off. He and his agent had been talking about getting a spin-off TV series about Mark when this series finishes.'

'Oooh,' nodded Soph. 'That would have been good.'

I kicked her under the table.

'He begged me to change my mind. But when I refused, he got nasty. The morning I came to Whitney High, he told me that he'd never loved me. It had all been for his career – being with me had all been about building his profile – and if I was killing him off, there was no point in us being together. I should have known, really. He was always making me go to parties and making sure we were photographed together. He'd have had *Star Secrets* photographing us in the bath if they were interested. That's the kind of person he is.'

'No wonder you didn't want to talk about him at the writing workshop,' I said.

Hollie smiled at me. 'When I got home that evening, he bundled me up into the attic and locked the door, saying he wouldn't let me out again until I changed my mind and rewrote the ending. I managed to escape out of the dormer window and climb down the drainpipe. All I had on me was the money in my purse. I couldn't use my credit cards because I knew the police would be able to trace where they were used. I headed back here, because it was the only place I could think of. And I knew Josh would never dream of looking for me here.'

She paused as Mrs Trotter shouted that our lunch was ready. Soph got up to collect it.

'But where have you been staying?' I asked.

'I checked into a bed and breakfast called the Tulip Inn, under the name of Mrs Green,' said Hollie. 'I had enough money on me to pay for that, but I had to sell my shoes to get money for food.'

'That's terrible!' cried Soph, peering under the table at Hollie's feet. 'Oooh, but your flip-flops are gorgeous. Very now.'

'Er, thanks,' said Hollie.

'You're welcome,' grinned Soph through a mouthful of cheese sandwich.

'But why didn't you just go to the police?' I asked. 'They could have protected you from Josh.'

'But then there would have been a national scandal, and all I wanted to do was finish the book on time. Josh can wait till I've finished. I know I've caused an awful lot of trouble, but I didn't know what else to do.'

Abs smiled at her. 'Your secret is totally safe with us. We'll help you in any way we can. We've got to get back to school, but we know where you're staying and we'll be in touch.'

As I reached under the table for my bag, I could have sworn I saw Amanda Hawkins staring at us through the window out of the corner of my eye. But when I looked up, there was no one there.

Chapter Six

I didn't see Abs and Soph again till drama class later that afternoon. The regional competition was only a week away and Time Lord was back to his usual nightmare self.

'Rosie Parker!' he shouted, as I walked across the stage and picked a pretend flower for what seemed like the billionth time. 'I've seen planks of wood with more acting ability than you. Go to the back of the hall and practise feeling old!'

Sighing, I shuffled off stage, passing a smirking Amanda Hawkins.

'So,' she drawled, 'not only are you as thick as a plank, now you're acting like one.'

OH, SOMEBODY CALL AN AMBULANCE, I THINK MY SIDES HAVE SPLIT FROM LAUGHING.

I stomped to the back of the hall, where Soph was bent over a sewing machine. Grumbling to myself, I practised walking up and down like an old person. Abs wandered over.

'I've been thinking,' she said. 'I reckon we should take it in turns to get food to Hollie so she can save money but not starve. It's not much, but at least it shows we care.'

'Sounds like a plan, Stan,' said Soph.

'Deffo,' I said. 'I'll do it tonight if you like. Mum's working late, and Nan will be holed up in the lounge watching a *Murder, She Wrote* DVD. I'll text you both later and let you know how I get on.'

'Don't forget Hollie's veggie,' said Abs. 'I remember that from the author info about her on her publisher's web site.'

'Oooh, good call, Saul,' I said.

We grinned at each other and high-fived.

'Rosie Parker!' shouted Time Lord. 'I don't remember it being in the script that the old lady spends any time gossiping with her friends or high-fiving! As for you, Miss McCoy, don't think I haven't got my eye on you. I want all the costumes finished by the end of the school day tomorrow, and this time, I don't want any of them to fall apart!'

I rolled my eyes at Abs and Soph, before toddling off in my old-lady walk once again.

* * *

Right, I told myself later. *Don't panic. You can so do this. All you have to do is make a nice vegetable casserole.* I stared at the recipe I'd downloaded from the Internet earlier. So, all I had to do was follow it. Easy-peasy – right?

Well, no, actually. Half an hour later, I dialled Abs's number for technical support:

Me: *Hellllllllllllllllllllllllllllp!*

Abs: *Calm down! What's up?*

Me: *I'm trying to make a vegetable casserole and it's all going wrong.*

Abs: *What's gone wrong?*

Me: *Well, first of all, we didn't have all the vegetables.*

Abs: *What vegetables did you need?*

Me: *Onions, garlic, potatoes, leeks, mushrooms, peppers and a courgette.*

Abs: *Right, so what have you got?*

Me: *An onion and a potato.*

Abs: *You're making a potato and onion casserole?*

Me: *[Crossly.] Yes.*

Abs: *Er, OK. Sounds . . . um . . . delicious.*

Me: *But that's not all!*

Abs: *It isn't?*

Me: *No. The recipe said to add tomato purée.*

Abs: *Right. And did you?*

Me: *No. We didn't have any. So I used tomato ketchup.*

Abs: *That's OK.*

Me: *Well, it would have been, except the ketchup wouldn't come out of the bottle, so I whacked it really hard . . .*

Abs: *And . . .*

Me: *And half the bottle came out! It's ruined.*

Abs: *[Letting out what seriously sounded like a laugh disguised as a cough.] Um, perhaps you should try making something else?*

I put the phone down and stared at it for a minute before picking it up and dialling again.

'Hello?' a voice answered.

'Hi,' I said. 'I'd like to order a large vegetable pizza, please.'

* * *

Half an hour later, I was ready to leave, clutching a scrummy-smelling pizza.

'I'm just popping out to see Abs, Nan,' I called. 'I won't be long.'

'OK,' she shouted back.

I opened the front door and started walking down the driveway.

'Rosie?'

I gave a startled jump. It was Mum. Sacré bleu! All that time I'd spent messing with the casserole meant that she'd got back before I left. Busted!

'Where are you going with that pizza?' she asked.

'Um, to see Abs,' I said.

'With a pizza?' asked Mum. 'Rosie, last time I checked there was no shortage of food at the Flynns'! I won't ask you again. Where are you going?'

I looked up at her concerned face and burst into tears. Mum reached out and took the pizza from me. 'Oh, honey. Come back inside and tell me what's going on.'

In between sobs, I poured out everything that had happened, from tracking Hollie down, to me, Abs and Soph deciding we would sneak her some food.

'I'm so sorry, Mum,' I said, wiping my eyes. 'I never meant to lie. It's just that we promised to keep it secret.'

Mum looked at me, her eyes all narrow and determined. 'Right,' she said, grabbing her car keys. 'Come on.'

'Where are we going?' I asked, surprised.

'To get Hollie,' she grinned at me. 'She can come here for dinner. After all, she's got to keep her strength up if she's going to finish that manuscript on time.'

* * *

Despite my initial worries about Mum's cooking – she's not what you'd call a natural in the kitchen – we had the most coolissimo evening *ever*. Hollie was pretty shocked when I turned up at the Tulip Inn with Mum in tow. But once I'd explained, the two of them were soon getting on like the best of friends. And I could tell Hollie was really touched that Mum wanted her to come and eat with us.

'She's lovely!' said Mum, as I helped her prepare dinner. 'Really charming. Such a nice, normal, down-to-earth person. You'd never guess she had all that money. She's even invited us to stay at her house when all this Josh stuff has blown over.'

'She and Nan seem to be getting on too!' I said.

'Oh, yes. In fact, she's looking at your nan's murder-mystery script. Nan thought Hollie might be able to give her some pointers.'

Zut alors! How embarrassing!

The doorbell rang.

'I'll get it,' I told Mum, heading for the front door. 'It's probably Abs or Soph – I texted them to say Hollie was round here . . .'

And then I stopped speaking, the words shrivelling on my lips. It wasn't Abs or Soph, it was Amanda Hawkins. She was wearing a bright pink tracksuit and hostility was crackling all around her.

'So . . .' she said, staring at me through narrowed eyes, 'I suppose you're feeling pretty proud of yourself, aren't you?'

'Er, no. Not really,' I said, totally bemused. 'Um, Amanda, I'm not being rude, but what do you want?'

She paused and examined a perfectly manicured nail.

'Does everyone know you're hiding Hollie Fraser?' she asked silkily.

NOOOOOOOOOOOOOOO! I *knew* I hadn't imagined seeing her outside Trotters – Dork-Hawkins must've been following us! OK, I had to keep calm. I could manage this.

'You wouldn't say anything,' I said.

'Wouldn't I?' She raised an eyebrow. 'I think a lot of people would be interested to know where she is.'

'Look, Amanda, I know we haven't always got on, but we've known each other a long time. Surely that counts for something?'

Seriously, it nearly killed me to say that – but I had no choice. I had to win her over.

I placed a hand on her velour sleeve. 'Please, Amanda.'

There was a pause while Amanda raked her eyes up and down me from head to toe. Then she jerked her hand away from mine.

'See you, Rosie,' she said and started to walk away.

'No!' I shouted after her. 'Please. Don't go. Look, come in and meet Hollie – then maybe you'll understand.'

Amanda stopped, and turned back to look at me. 'OK,' she said. 'Five minutes.' And, brushing past me, she walked into the house.

Chapter Seven

'You did WHAT?' shouted Abs. 'You told Amanda Hawkins about . . .'

'Shhh!' I pleaded, looking around me at the school canteen. Fortunately, in a canteen packed full of chattering school kids, it's pretty tough to work out what the person next to you is saying, let alone overhear someone at a different table.

'But why?' said Soph. 'Why would you tell Amanda Hawkins? Have you lost your *mind*?'

I sighed. 'I told her because she already knew.'

'WHAT?' screeched Abs again.

'Keep your voice down!' I said. 'Do you want the whole world to know?'

'I don't need to let the whole world know,' she said. 'You've done it for us, by telling Amanda Witchface Hawkins. I mean, why don't you just get a megaphone and announce it to the whole canteen?'

'If you'd just let me explain,' I said crossly.

'Go ahead,' said Abs, sitting back and folding her arms.

'Right,' I said. 'Well, basically, me, Mum, Nan and,' I lowered my voice and looked around me, 'H.'

'Who?' said Soph.

'H!' I said.

'Who's H?' asked Soph.

Honestly, sometimes I wonder if all that fashion has seriously affected her mind. 'Hollie,' I mouthed.

'Ohhhhh!' she said. 'Got you.'

'Anyway, the four of us were at my house. When there was a knock on the door, I answered it, thinking it was going to be one of you two, but it wasn't. It was Amanda Hawkins. And she stood there, bold as brass, and told me that she knew that H was inside and that she was going to tell.'

'Nooooo!' said Soph.

'Yes,' I said. 'Anyway, I managed to persuade her to come in. I left her in the hallway while I went to explain to H what had happened. She said we had no choice. She would have to explain everything to Amanda and appeal to her better nature.'

'Ha! As if she's got one,' sniffed Abs.

'I know. That's what I said,' I nodded at Abs. 'But it was the only option. So I went out and got Amanda and H told her everything.'

'And then what happened?' asked Soph.

'She stood up, shook H's hand and said she'd keep her secret,' I said.

'As if!' scoffed Abs.

'No, I really think she meant it,' I said. 'She even said she was sorry for threatening to tell. Maybe she's not such a witch after all?'

'You know what?' said Soph, 'I'm starting to see a new side to Amanda Hawkins. Becky told me this morning that she saw her in the library, reading the papers on the Internet. Who'd have thought Amanda Hawkins had an interest in current affairs?'

'Current affairs my elbow!' said Abs. 'She was probably reading her horoscope!'

'Talk of the devil,' hissed Soph, as Amanda walked up to us.

'Hi guys,' she said, smiling sweetly as she pulled up a chair. 'I just wanted to say that I hope your Auntie H is doing OK, Rosie, and that she gets her . . . *project* done on time.'

'Er, thanks,' I said, trying not to look too shocked at the sight of Amanda Hawkins being nice to us. 'I think she will.'

'Cool. You don't mind if I eat my lunch with you guys, do you?' she said, pulling her sandwiches out of her bag. 'Anyway, so how are you all?'

She glanced over at Abs. 'I love what you've done with your hair, Abigail,' she said.

Abs's mouth fell open so much, her jaw almost hit the table.

✳ ✳ ✳

Later that afternoon, me and Abs were in the toilets after our latest drama rehearsal. I was still recovering from feeling the full force of Time Lord's wrath. Being told that you have less acting ability than a slab of meat hanging in a butcher's shop does nothing for a girl's ego, let me tell you.

'I'm still not convinced we can trust Amanda,' she said. 'This sudden butter-wouldn't-melt attitude just doesn't ring true.'

'As long as she keeps her lips zipped, that's all that matters,' I said, as we headed into the cubicles.

We fell silent as the door opened and somebody came in.

'What is *up* with Amanda?' came Lara Neils' familiar voice from over by the sinks.

'I know!' said a voice that could only belong to Keira Roberts. 'Did you see her at lunchtime, sucking up to the tragic triplets? She was practically kissing Dozy Rosie's bum!'

'Well, if she carries on like that, I will seriously consider not hanging around with her any more. She's obviously cashed in her cool for a one-way ticket to Loserville.'

They giggled and the toilet door clanged shut behind them. Me and Abs emerged from our cubicles.

'Wowissimo!' said Abs, her eyebrows disappearing into her hairline. 'Maybe I've misjudged Amanda Hawkins after all.'

We walked out into the corridor and bumped straight into – guess who? – Amanda Hawkins.

'Just the people I was looking for,' she smiled. 'Rosie, I thought your old lady was so much better today. You had me convinced.'

'Try telling Time Lord that,' I muttered. 'Honestly, I could come back in sixty years' time, when I actually *am* an old lady, walk across the stage, pick a pretend flower and he *still* wouldn't find me convincing.'

'Ha, ha, ha!' laughed Amanda. 'Rosie Parker, you are hilarious!'

'Er, thanks,' I said.

'Anyway,' she said, linking arms with me and Abs and lowering her voice conspiratorially, 'I wanted to ask you, where's *Auntie H* going to be on the night of the drama competition?'

'I don't know,' I said.

'Well, I was thinking,' said Amanda, squeezing my arm, 'wouldn't it be cool if she could come to the competition? In disguise, obviously. I mean, you never know, she might see how talented we all are and make sure we're cast in her next movie.'

'You wish!' laughed Abs. 'Seriously, though, there's no way we could risk her being in such a public place. Even in disguise. Anyway, isn't she spending the night at yours, Rosie, so she can get on with her writing in peace?'

Abruptly, Amanda let go of my arm. 'Oh,' she said, shrugging. 'Well, it was just an idea. I'll see you tomorrow.'

As we walked down the corridor, I glanced

back over my shoulder to say goodbye. Amanda was watching us walk away, her hands on her hips and her eyes narrowed. She looked like the old Amanda. I went to wave goodbye but she was turning away, pulling her phone out of her bag. I felt a flicker of unease. I couldn't shake the image of Amanda's narrowed eyes. Something was wrong. I just wasn't sure what. There was only one thing for it – I was going to have to go back for a chat with her to reassure myself that everything was OK.

'Abs, I've left my English homework assignment in my locker. I'll catch you up, OK?' I said, and turned back.

I hurried along the corridor. As I turned the corner by the lockers, I stopped dead as I heard Amanda's voice. Who was she talking to? I peered round the corner. Amanda was leaning against the wall, her back turned to me, talking into her mobile. I froze as I heard her ask for the number of the *Daily Gossip*.

What? Why would Amanda want the number

of the *Daily Gossip?* It was the biggest tabloid in the country. I listened as hard as I could.

'Hello?' she was saying. 'I have a huge story for you . . . yes . . . it's about Hollie Fraser. Who should I speak to? The news editor? OK . . . yes, yes . . . I'll hold.'

She couldn't be about to say what I thought she was going to say. She *couldn't*. She *wouldn't*. I must be wrong. She must be about to give them a red herring. Yes, that would be it. *She'll probably tell them that she's spotted Hollie in Edinburgh or something. Send them on a wild goose chase*, I thought.

'Hello? Is that the news editor?' Amanda's voice rang out down the empty corridor. 'How much would you pay for a story that led you to the whereabouts of Hollie Fraser? . . . Really? That much? Wow! In that case, if you'd like to meet me at Borehurst Town Hall tomorrow night at ten o'clock, I'll take you to her myself.'

NOOOOO!

Chapter Eight

I texted Abs and Soph – **Crisis meeting at my house NOW!** – and called Hollie, asking her to come over.

Half an hour later we were all gathered round the kitchen table with Nan and Mum. A plate of chocolate muffins was left completely untouched (which, believe me, is totally unheard-of in the Parker household) as I filled everyone in on what I had heard of Amanda's conversation.

'I *knew* it was too good to be true!' breathed Soph when I ground to a halt. 'She must have been working out which newspaper to sell the story to when she was in the library the other day. I should have put two and two together sooner.'

'Don't be silly, Soph,' I said, 'It's not your fault. I just can't believe we fell for her "new best friend" act.'

'I know!' agreed Abs. 'I think she really thought that if she kept us sweet, we might persuade Hollie to come and watch the drama competition, and she'd take one look at Amanda prancing around on stage and instantly whisk her off to make her a mega Hollywood star.'

'Totally ridiculous!' I butted in. 'You'd never catch me thinking anything like that.'

Abs looked at me. 'So Rosie, you're telling us you've never, ever got carried away at the idea of meeting a celeb and imagined yourself becoming best friends with them?'

I could feel myself going as pink as Mum's stilettos. 'I don't know what you mean,' I said, indignantly.

Abs gave my arm an affectionate squeeze. 'Of

course you don't. Anyway, I reckon it was only when she found out that Hollie definitely wasn't going to be there that she decided to go to the papers.'

'But where on earth would she get the idea to sell the story?' said Mum. 'She's just a schoolgirl.'

'I expect it was when I told her about Josh, and how much money someone could make from revealing how the book ends,' said Hollie sadly.

I stared at her, horrified. 'So now she knows how the book ends *and* where you are! So even if you move on from Borehurst, she'll still be able to spill the beans on how the *Dirty Tricks* series ends. I'm so sorry, Hollie. It's all my fault. If I'd just bluffed it out when she said she knew you were here, Amanda would never have known anything!'

I couldn't bear it. I burst into tears. Hollie jumped up and ran round the table, enveloping me in the most ginormous hug.

'It's not your fault,' she said. 'It's no one's fault. To be honest, I'm amazed I've been able to get away with it for so long. If the game's up, then the game's up. It's a fair cop, guv!' She laughed shakily.

I couldn't believe she was being so brave and I sobbed noisily into her jumper. Abs, Soph and Mum jumped up and threw their arms around us. Seriously, you could hardly move for the love in the room.

Nan shook her head in disbelief. 'I can't believe you're all about to give up so easily. We're more than a match for that silly, spiteful little schoolgirl.' She leaned in across the table. 'Now, if you'd all like to stop hugging for five minutes, I have a plan . . .'

* * *

The next morning, the three of us were sitting on a bench in the schoolyard, when Amanda Hawkins came rushing over, her ponytail swinging behind her.

'Hi, guys,' she said, smiling at us all. 'Is *Auntie H* still staying at yours tonight, Rosie?'

'She most certainly is,' said Soph, nudging me in the ribs. 'Isn't she, Rosie?'

'Yes,' I said. 'She's pretty close to finishing her project, I think.'

'That's brilliant,' Amanda smiled sweetly.

'But it means we won't be able to stay long at the party after the competition tonight,' I added. 'We need to get home and check on her.'

'I won't be able to stay for long either,' said Amanda. 'I, um, have to meet someone.'

Me, Abs and Soph exchanged glances.

'That's nice,' said Abs. 'Anyone we know?'

'No, just a friend,' Amanda breezed. 'Anyway, guys, have to run. See you later.'

'*Witch*,' hissed Soph as we watched her run across the field towards Keira Roberts and Lara Neils. Judging by the smirks they were sending in our direction, Amanda Hawkins had wasted no time filling them in.

✳ ✳ ✳

That evening, we piled on to a coach and set off for the regional drama competition. Time Lord stood beside the driver, giving us all last-minute advice.

'Now, remember, boys and girls, the eyes of the world are on me – I mean, you – tonight. So shine, people, shine! And if any of you get nervous, then just look at Amanda, and take confidence from what I am sure will be another amazing performance.'

I grimaced at Soph, who crossed her eyes and stuck her fingers down her throat.

'Feeling sick again, Miss McCoy?' asked Time Lord, frowning at us from the front of the coach.

'Sorry, Mr Lord,' said Soph. 'I think it's travel sickness.'

The two of us giggled as the coach pulled into the car park at Borehurst town hall and we headed inside. The windows of our dressing room were all covered with black material so we could change in private. Everyone was getting excited, clambering into their costumes and crowding round the mirror. We were the last school to perform, and we could hear applause and laughter out front as the other competitors acted their socks off. Time Lord had made it clear we weren't allowed to peek.

'Theatre is all about smoke and mirrors. If anyone sees you peering round the curtain, it spoils the illusion. It's all about magic, people – *magic*!'

I had butterflies in my stomach. No, scratch that, not butterflies – it was more like a herd of hippos stampeding through my insides. But it wasn't about the competition. I couldn't stop thinking about Nan's plan.

'Relax, Rosie,' said Abs.

'How can I relax?' I asked.

'It's fine. It's all under control,' she said for the millionth time.

Time Lord appeared in the doorway. 'This is it, people. We're on. Break a leg!'

Soph was standing in the wings, making last-minute costume adjustments.

'Feeling nervous?' she asked.

'Not really!' I said.

Which was kind of true. In fact, it was totally

true. I was beyond nervous. Either everything went to plan and all this worked out, or it didn't and it would be a complete disaster.

Soph winked at me. 'Rosie, if we pull this off, we deserve an award!'

'Rosie!' hissed Time Lord. 'What are you doing? You're on!' He shoved me on to the stage, pushing me so hard that he cricked my back, so it was absolutely no problem to walk like an old lady. I winced as I bent awkwardly to pick up the flower. As I staggered back into the wings, rubbing my spine, Time Lord grabbed me.

'Rosie Parker, that performance was inspired!' he said.

'And I can honestly say, Mr Lord, it was all thanks to you,' I answered truthfully, trying to ignore the shooting pains in my back.

I headed back to the dressing room, where everyone was waiting. A few minutes later, applause broke out and Amanda Hawkins burst into the dressing room with Time Lord right on her heels.

'That was your best performance yet,' he told her. Usually, Amanda would bask in his praise, but today, she just smiled smugly and started taking off her heavy stage make-up. Me and Abs started doing the same. Time Lord paced up and down the room, muttering under his breath, while we waited for the results to be announced.

Suddenly, a voice crackled over the loudspeaker in the dressing room. I jumped and everyone fell silent. They were about to announce the winner. Time Lord stuffed his fist into his mouth.

'Well, it's been an amazing night, I'm sure you'll agree,' said the voice. There was a deafening round of applause from the audience and shouts of 'Hear, hear!'

The voice continued, 'But there can only be one winner. So please give a huge round of applause to tonight's winning school . . .' The voice paused. I glanced at Time Lord, who looked like he was about to be sick. '. . . Whitney High!'

'Yeeeeeeeeeeeeeeeeeeeeeeeeeeessssssssssssssssss!' shouted Time Lord, punching the air. He ran to the dressing-room door, pushing everyone out of his way as he rushed on to the stage. Me, Soph and Abs made our way on to the stage just in time to watch as he grabbed the trophy out of the judge's hands.

'I'd like to thank the original cast of *Doctor Who*, who encouraged me to progress from playing a Cyberman to become the playwright you see before you,' he gushed. 'I'd like to thank my parents for always believing in me. They're here tonight. Mum, Dad, take a bow. I'd also like to thank my dog, Casper, for giving me unconditional love. Thank you all so much. Thank you and goodnight!'

The judge whispered something in his ear.

'Oh,' said Time Lord. 'And I'd like to thank the pupils at Whitney High too.'

GEE, THANKS, TIME LORD. DON'T DO US ANY FAVOURS, WILL YOU?

Abs nudged me, 'Rosie! We have to go! Amanda's just left!'

We grabbed Soph and the three of us ran for the exit. On stage, Time Lord had sunk to his knees. He was kissing the trophy and wiping his eyes. The bemused judge was patting his shoulder while trying to remove him from the stage.

The three of us pelted to the car park, where Mum and Nan were already waiting for us, the car engine running.

'You were all great tonight,' Mum beamed as we clambered into the car, seriously out of breath.

'Yes, yes!' Nan said impatiently. 'Praise can wait. Now drive, woman, *drive!*'

* * *

A hair-raisingly short journey later, we pulled into our driveway. Amanda Hawkins was already there, ringing the doorbell. A guy dressed in a sharp suit was standing next to her. He had a camera slung over his shoulder. We climbed out of the car quickly.

'Amanda,' I said. 'What are you doing here?'

Amanda narrowed her eyes, 'Just open the door, Rosie – the game's up.'

'What game?' I asked her. 'I don't know what you mean.'

'You know exactly what I mean. This is Tony, from the *Daily Gossip.*' She smiled, maliciously. 'He's here to see *Auntie H.*'

She looked at me triumphantly and I felt my stomach lurch.

Nan stepped forward. 'Oh, *Auntie H.* Why didn't you say so, dear?' She put her key in the lock and opened the front door. 'Come in.'

Amanda looked at her as if she couldn't believe her stupidity. Then, brushing past us, she marched into the house, Tony hot on her heels. Taking her time, she strolled along the hallway. You could so tell she was relishing every moment. Keeping her eyes on me, she threw open the door to the lounge.

'Tony, meet Hollie Fraser!' she announced, gesturing at the dark-haired woman who was sitting on the sofa, her back to us, papers spread out around her.

'Hollie Fraser?' I laughed. 'What are you talking about, Amanda?'

'I've told you, Rosie, the game's up.' She turned to the journalist. 'I hope you've got your camera ready.'

She walked towards the dark-haired woman, who hadn't moved and was still sitting with her back to us. 'Come on,' Amanda's voice hardened. 'There's no point in trying to hide any more. It's time for your close-up, Hollie. Why don't you give the nice journalist your best smile?'

The figure on the sofa finally turned round. Tony darted forward with his camera at the ready, then stopped.

'Is this some kind of joke?' he asked.

'W-w-what?' said Amanda. She pushed past the journalist, then stopped dead as a complete stranger stood up from the sofa.

'I'm sorry,' said the woman. 'I didn't realise you were talking to me. All this talk of Hollie completely confused me.' She gestured to a pile of papers on the floor. 'You'll have to excuse the mess. I've been working on my project.'

Amanda was looking stunned. The woman

beamed. 'I should introduce myself. I'm Auntie H.'

'I don't know what's going on here,' said the journalist, 'and to be honest, I really don't care. But you, young lady,' he said, pointing at Amanda, 'have completely wasted my evening.' He turned and stalked out of the room.

'But I don't understand,' said Amanda, looking as if she was about to cry.

'The only thing you need to understand,' said Nan, sticking her head out into the hallway to make sure the journalist had really gone, 'is that Hollie Fraser is somewhere you'll never find her. And don't even think about going to the papers with the ending of the *Dirty Tricks* series. No paper will touch you after tonight. The *Daily Gossip* will take care of that!'

'You can't do this to me,' shouted Amanda. 'You . . . arggghhh!' Her voice rose to a scream. 'Put me down!'

Nan had hoisted her up on to her shoulder and was carrying her out of the room as if she were a naughty toddler.

'Put me down,' she shouted. 'Put me down!'

The lounge door slammed, cutting her off. Then the door opened again and Nan reappeared, brushing her hands.

'That's what we do with rubbish,' she said firmly. 'Throw it out.'

There was a shocked moment, then we all started to laugh. I ran over and gave Nan a huge-issimo hug.

'You were brilliant!' I told her.

'Totally coolissimo,' added Soph.

'Let's not forget to thank Auntie H,' said Mum, smiling at her friend, Christina – a fellow member of the Banana Splits. Christina grinned and gave a little bow.

'It was my pleasure,' she said. 'Any time. When Liz told me what was going on, and said you needed a decoy to fool the *Daily Gossip*, I was only too happy to help! I'm a huge Hollie Fraser fan.'

Abs started laughing again. 'Did you *see* the look on Amanda's face! Classic!'

Chapter Nine

A few days later, I was in my room when my computer beeped. It was an email from Hollie. Excitedly, I clicked on it:

Dearest Rosie,

I wanted you (and Abs, Soph, your mum and, of course, your nan!) to be the first to know that the book is finally finished and is now safely with my publisher. Thank you; I'd never have finished it without your help.

I'm holding a press conference tomorrow at

Hotel Londonia to explain my disappearance. I guess it's time to tell the world I haven't been kidnapped! I'd love it if you could all be there. Your names are on the guest list and I really hope you can make it. I'm looking forward to catching up with you all.

Hope to see you tomorrow.

Much love

Hollie xxx

Wow! A press conference! Coolissimo! Nothing would stop me from going. I couldn't wait!

✳ ✳ ✳

We were all totally over-excited the next day when we walked into the hotel. Everywhere I looked there were lavish flower arrangements and baskets of fruit. Total glam-a-rama!

We followed the signs for the press conference and gave our names at the door. The atmosphere inside was hushed and expectant. As Nan, Mum,

Abs and Soph squeezed into our seats, I stood at the side, trying to take in every little detail. The room was packed with journalists holding dictaphones or pens and notebooks. Photographers jostled for the best spots at the side of the room. At the back, there were loads of cameramen peering through their lenses. There was a raised platform at the front with a table and a row of empty chairs on it.

'Excuse me,' said a voice. 'Don't I know you from somewhere?'

Zut alors! It was Tony, the journalist from the *Daily Gossip! Oh, no. He mustn't recognise me*, I thought urgently.

'Um, er, no,' I said. 'I don't think so.'

He looked at me suspiciously. 'Are you sure? I could have sworn we'd met.'

'Er, no, zorry, I am French,' I said, putting on a fake accent. 'Pleaze, if you will, er – 'ow you say? – excusez moi.'

It was only when I sat down next to Mum that it occurred to me that it didn't matter if he did recognise me. Hollie Fraser was about to tell everyone what had really happened and there was no need to lie any more!

OOPS!

Just then a door at the front of the room opened and Hollie walked in, flanked by a man and a woman. Hollie looked totally gorgeous, dressed in skinny jeans, a halterneck top and her trademark Fabconis. She walked to one of the empty chairs and sat down.

The man walked to the front of the room. 'Ladies and gentlemen, Hollie Fraser has prepared a statement. There will be time for questions afterwards. Thank you.'

Just then, the door opened again and Josh Stevens rushed in.

'What's *he* doing here?' hissed Soph.

We watched, open-mouthed, as he hurried over to the empty chair next to Hollie and gave her hand a squeeze. She smiled at him, and he rubbed her shoulders, dropping a kiss on to her neck.

'Ewww!' Soph was squirming in her seat. 'How can she bear to let him touch her?'

What was going on? Surely she couldn't have forgiven him. Not after everything he'd put her through! Nooo! I couldn't bear it.

Hollie leant forward and began to speak. 'Ladies and gentlemen, I would like to thank each and every one of you for coming today. I realise what a fuss my disappearance has caused. I would particularly like to thank Josh.' She paused, turned and smiled at him. He reached out and kissed her hand.

'Ahhhhhhh,' sighed the female reporter behind me.

'Ewwww!' chorused me, Abs and Soph.

Hollie turned and smiled at the room. 'I'd particularly like to thank Josh for being here today. You see, it's pretty brave of him to turn up, since he was the one who tried to kidnap me.'

A shocked gasp rippled around the room. For an instant, Josh looked pretty shocked too, but then he stood up, a professional smile on his lips. 'Darling!' he said, giving a silvery laugh. 'I think you're confused. It must be the shock of what you've been through.'

'Yes, that's it,' the reporter in front of me, nodded wisely. 'Shock. As if Josh Stevens would kidnap anyone.'

The girl next to her giggled. 'Well, he can kidnap me any time he likes. He's gorgeous!'

'I'm not confused, Josh,' said Hollie. 'I know exactly what happened.'

Josh now had his hand on Hollie's elbow. 'Ladies and gentlemen, I hope you will excuse us. I think we need to get Hollie to a doctor.'

This was terrible! How the crusty old grandads was Hollie going to make anyone believe her side of the story? It was her word against Josh's. He looked totally reasonable standing there, his face full of concern. I looked around to see people nodding and looking sympathetic.

'The poor thing,' I heard the female reporter whisper, as Josh took hold of a struggling Hollie and started walking her to the door. 'All this success has obviously been too much for her. She must be having some kind of breakdown.'

Without thinking, I stood up.

'It's *true!*' I shouted. Josh stopped manhandling Hollie and turned to see who was speaking. I glared at him. 'Josh tried to kidnap Hollie!'

'Sit down, kid,' scoffed one of the reporters. Josh raised his eyebrows at the room and shrugged in an I-don't-know-kids-today kind of way. The female reporter in front of me giggled.

Angry tears were pouring down my face as I looked around the room. I had to get them to believe me. I had to.

'None of you think I'm telling the truth, but I am,' I practically shrieked. 'Josh is only interested in his career. I mean, anyone can see that. You only had to see the press conference he gave just after Hollie went missing.' I looked at Nan, who winked at me encouragingly. 'Did he talk about how much he loved her, or how worried he was for her safety? No. He went on and on about how much he was looking forward to playing Mark in the next movie. And you know what? When the book comes out, you'll see that Hollie's telling the truth . . .'

'Hang on a minute,' said a reporter, turning round in his chair to look at me. 'I remember watching that press conference and thinking it was odd that Josh didn't show more emotion. I put it down to stress. But maybe the kid's got a point.'

'She's a schoolgirl, for heaven's sake,' said Josh, still holding on to Hollie's elbow. 'Are you really going to listen to her?'

The reporter looked from him to me. 'You said something about us believing Hollie once the book came out?'

'Yes!' I said, wiping my nose attractively on my sleeve.

'I don't know what she's talking about,' said Josh, still holding on to Hollie's elbow.

Something had changed in the reporter's eyes. 'Does that mean Josh's character dies in the book?'

'Yes!' I said.

There was a collective gasp from around the room.

'No, he doesn't!' said Josh, but the blood had drained from his face and he'd started to shake.

'Yes, he does!' I practically shouted. 'And you were so angry and worried about what the effect would be on your career, you tried to kidnap Hollie to make her rewrite the ending.'

'I believe you,' said the reporter.

'So do I,' said the journalist next to him.

'And me,' said another. All around the room, people were nodding.

'I . . . er . . . I . . .' stuttered Josh. Suddenly he let go of Hollie, stepped off the stage and bolted for the door, but two policemen blocked his way.

'Josh Stevens,' one of them said. 'I've got some questions I'd like you to answer down at the station, please.'

As he was escorted from the room, the reporter behind me said, 'Looks like they'll have to find someone new to play Mark Green.'

'Definitely,' agreed the woman next to him. 'The only place his career is going is straight down the toilet.'

'I never thought he was that attractive, anyway,' said the female reporter in front of me.

Relieved, I plonked myself back down in my chair, then jumped to my feet again straight away as the horrible realisation hit me that in my attempt to show Josh up for what he really was, I'd only gone and given away the ending of the whole *Dirty Tricks* series to a roomful of journalists, photographers and cameramen! Nervously, I cleared my throat and said, 'Um, I realise I kind of told you all what happened at the end of the book. Would you mind . . . um . . . well, not revealing it?'

There was silence and then most of the room burst into laughter.

'Not reveal it?' chortled the female journalist in front of me. 'Not publish the story of the year? You're having a laugh, aren't you?'

Then the reporter who'd said he believed me stood up. 'I've got a fifteen-year-old daughter, and she would never forgive me if I gave away the ending,' he said. Quite a few other people nodded in agreement.

'So?' said the female journalist. 'You're a reporter – it's your job. She'll get over it.'

There were a few murmurs of 'Hear, hear,' and 'She's right.'

I glanced over at Hollie, who was sitting upright, watching the goings-on nervously. The reporter shook his head at the female journalist, before continuing. 'While it may look like the story of the year, can you imagine the uproar from parents if we disclose the ending and ruin the book for children all over the country? It could seriously damage our circulation. The book isn't even due to come out for another few months.' The reporter looked around the room. People were starting to nod and whisper amongst themselves. 'I can't believe I'm about to say this, but I suggest we don't run the story.'

'No way!' said the female journalist. 'My editor would kill me!'

'So don't tell your editor,' said the reporter. 'What editors don't know can't hurt them.'

A few people laughed and nodded.

'I suggest we put it to the vote,' the reporter said. 'Those who think we should keep quiet about the ending, raise your hands.'

I held my breath as, one by one, journalists, photographers and cameramen started raising their hands. Soon everyone, including Nan, had their hands in the air. Well, everyone apart from the female journalist in front of me, who was sitting with her arms folded, tapping her foot impatiently. Nan leant forward and prodded her with her umbrella.

'Ever heard the saying, "if you can't beat 'em, join 'em"?' she asked. The female journalist glared at her, before tutting and sulkily raising her hand like everyone else.

The nice reporter turned to Hollie. 'It looks like your secret's safe with us,' he said and winked at her. 'Trust me, I'm a journalist.'

Three things not to do when a famous author asks you to stand up and take a bow at a press conference:

1. Squeal and clap excitedly.
2. Wave into the nearest TV camera and shout,

'In your face, Amanda Hawkins!'

3. Miss your seat when you sit back down and end up sprawled on the floor with your knickers on show to the whole world!

Chapter Ten

A few days later, me, Abs and Soph were walking
down the school corridor on our way to assembly.
It was taking us an age to get anywhere, as every
few minutes someone would stop us, saying, 'Way
to go!' or 'Nice one!' And, to be honest, we weren't
in any hurry – assemblies don't exactly rock my
world, if you know what I mean. In last week's
assembly, we'd had to sit through a slide-show of
Meanie Greenie's recent trip to Hong Kong.
Yawnsville or what?

Hollie's story had made national headlines and

the three of us were now total heroes at school. I don't know if anyone would have been quite so impressed if they'd realised I'd accidentally given away the ending of the *Dirty Tricks* series to a roomful of journalists.

Suddenly Time Lord appeared in a whirlwind of long coat, scarf and trainers.

'Ladies,' he said, 'may I just say how enchanting you're all looking today?'

Soph choked in shock and spat out a mouthful of cheese-and-onion crisps all over Time Lord's scarf. We stared, gobsmacked, as he didn't even flinch.

'Delightful, delightful,' he murmured, absent-mindedly wiping it off.

'Um, are you OK, Time – I mean, Mr Lord?' I asked.

'Oh, yes, yes, I'm absolutely fine.' Time Lord glanced both ways down the corridor, then leaned over.

'Rosie,' he whispered.

Slightly alarmed, I stepped back against the wall.

'Yes?' I said.

'I wanted to give you this.' Once again, he checked the corridor in both directions before pulling a large envelope out of his coat and thrusting it at me. 'I think you'll know what to do with it.'

He touched his finger to his nose and winked.

'Ewwww!' said Soph.

Smiling at the three of us, Time Lord whisked off down the corridor, disappearing into the assembly hall.

The three of us blinked at each other.

'What. Was. *That*. About?' I said.

'Only one way to find out,' said Abs, nodding at the envelope. 'Open it.'

Waggling my eyebrows at Abs and Soph, I tore open the package and pulled out a humungous pile of paper, neatly bound together. I peered at the writing on the front.

'"A screenplay by Tim Lord",' I read out loud.

'*What?*' squawked Soph. 'Why's he given you that?'

'I dunno,' I shrugged. 'Maybe he thinks I'm best friends with Hollie now, so I'll pass it on. And obviously she'll be so impressed with his talent that he'll be whisked off to Hollywood. Dream on! I haven't even heard from Hollie since the press conference.'

And, if I'm honest, this bothered me a tiny bit. It's not like I expected us to become best buddies or anything but, let's face it, if it hadn't been for me, Abs and Soph, she'd never have finished her book. Plus, let's not forget that I managed to make a whole roomful of the press believe her. And everyone knows they're some of the most cynical people in the world. (OK, I might have slipped up a tiny little bit when I accidentally gave away the ending of the *Dirty Tricks* series. But everyone makes mistakes, don't they? And I put it right in the end, and that's what counts.) I mean, it wouldn't have exactly killed her to show a bit more gratitude, would it?

Abs grabbed the screenplay out of my hands. 'This I've got to see!' she said, starting to read the first page.

'No way!' she giggled after a second. 'Read this!'
She held the first page up for me and Soph to see.

WORTH THE WAIT

A play by Tim Lord

Synopsis:

Tom Lourdes is a handsome and incredibly
talented young man whose life long dream has
been to be an actor. He started his career in a blaze
of glory, appearing in what was to become one of
the all-time biggest TV series. But Tom selflessly
decided to turn his back on shallowness, fame,
fortune and money, to teach children the craft of
acting instead – hoping to discover a light as bright
as his own could have been. But all that was to
change one day when a writer walked into his
school and saw him at work. She knew immediately
that this man belonged on the big screen, sharing
his talent with the world. She also knew, beyond a
shadow of doubt, that although she was already

dating a huge movie star, she had fallen utterly and helplessly head-over-heels in love with this brooding drama teacher. Would she be able to persuade him to leave teaching, to return to a world he thought he'd left behind? And could they ever be more to each other than writer and actor?

Me, Soph and Abs looked at each other and cracked up.

'Is he for real?' shrieked Soph, who was laughing so hard she had to hold on to the wall for support.

'I know!' I spluttered. 'That's got to be the funniest thing I've ever heard. I can't wait to read the whole play!'

The three of us collapsed on the floor, helpless with laughter.

'Rosie Parker, Abigail Flynn and Sophie McCoy! Will you stop mucking around and get in here *now*!' Mrs Oldman was standing in the school corridor, glaring at us, holding the door to the assembly hall open.

'Sorry, Mrs Oldham,' I said. The three of us scrambled to our feet, wiping our eyes, and hurried along the corridor. We walked past her into the hall and stopped dead. Everyone in the room stood up and started clapping and cheering.

'What's going on?' I asked, looking at Mrs Oldham in confusion.

'There's someone here to see you,' she smiled, nodding towards the front of the hall. I followed her gaze and gasped as I saw Hollie Fraser grinning at us.

'Well, girls,' said Mrs Oldham. If I didn't know better, I could have sworn she winked at us. 'What are you waiting for?'

As we walked up to the front of the assembly hall, the whole room went crazy. People were slapping our backs, and even Keira Roberts and Lara Neils were leaning forward, trying to shake our hands. Amanda Hawkins stood next to them, scowling. Word had got out about how she'd tried to expose Hollie. Let's just say she was now about as popular as the school canteen would be if it started serving frogs' legs on toast.

As we got to the front of the hall and climbed up on to the stage, Hollie reached out and hugged us, then turned to face the hall.

'Hi, everyone,' she said.

No one took a blind bit of notice. Not surprising really – the noise level was louder than Mum's tribute band, and believe me, that's noisy.

She tried again. 'Er, hello . . .'

Mrs Oldham stepped forward. 'WILL YOU ALL JUST SHUT UP!'

Everyone jumped about three feet into the air, but at least the room fell silent and people sat down.

'Um, thanks, Mrs Oldham,' Hollie said. 'Well, I'm here to say a huge thank you to these three girls. Without their help, I'd never have got the final book in the *Dirty Tricks* series finished. They're a credit to Whitney High.'

There were more cheers, but Hollie held her hand up for silence.

'I only wish that everyone had been as supportive. Things could have turned out very differently if I hadn't had these three on my side.' She was looking straight at Amanda Hawkins, who had gone bright scarlet – practically the same colour as Hollie's red Fabconis.

Everyone in the hall was whispering and nudging each other. Sacré bleu, it almost made me feel sorry for Amanda. Hollie held up her hand to hush everyone. 'However, I have received a heartfelt apology, and I'm prepared to forgive and forget.' She smiled at Amanda, who had gone an even more lobstery colour. I grinned at Soph and Abs. It was great to see Amanda looking flustered for a change.

Hollie winked at the three of us before carrying on. 'Anyway, as I was saying, I just really wanted to thank Rosie, Abs and Soph – and not forgetting Rosie's Mum and Nan. And I couldn't think of a better way of doing it than by dedicating the final book in the series to them.'

I gaped at her, totally gobsmacked. No *way*! The most eagerly anticipated book ever to be written was going to be dedicated to us! People all over the world would read it and wonder who we were and what made us so special. Oooh! Perhaps a journalist would read it and track us down and do a big story on us, and make us famous. And girls all over the world would wish they had friends and family as cool as us . . .

I snapped back to the present, as Abs and Soph jumped on me in a massivo hug – practically knocking me to the floor – while the rest of the school clapped and cheered.

* * *

A few months later, I got home from school to find Mum and Nan waiting for me at the kitchen table.

'Rosie! At last! Where have you been?' said Nan, drumming her fingers on the table, impatiently.

'Sorry, Nan,' I said. 'It's this new-fangled concept called school. Kids go there to do this thing called *learning* every weekday from nine to half-past three. Didn't they have it in your day?'

'Your school could do with teaching you some manners, young lady,' Nan said, pretending to glare at me. 'Now if you can find a moment in between sarcastic comments, we have something for you.'

'What?' I said. Mum was practically wriggling off her seat with excitement as she reached under the table and pulled out a package. What the crusty old grandads was going on?

Sacré bleu! I thought. *Please don't let it be the mini-me outfit Mum was talking about last week.*

Mum had decided it would be really cute if I went to one of her gigs dressed like her, as a backing singer. I thought I'd managed to get out of it by telling her I needed to concentrate on my school work. But maybe not. I eyed the package suspiciously. Mum pushed it towards me.

'Come on, Rosie,' she said. 'Don't keep us in suspense! Open it!'

I turned the package over, nervously. It was marked Warren Books. Oooh, la, la! It was from Hollie's publishers! Hands shaking, I ripped it open. There it was – the final book in the *Dirty Tricks* series:

Over and Out. It wasn't even going to be in the shops for another month. I stared at the trademark black cover with *Dirty Tricks* printed across the top in huge gold letters. Then, my heart pumping, I opened the book and read the dedication:

To the fab five: Rosie, Abs, Soph, Liz and Pam

This book would never have been finished without you. I will never forget how much I (and everyone else who loves this series) owe you. You are truly five in a million.

Thank you always, Hollie.

I stared at it, blinking back tears. This was quite possibly the coolest thing that ever happened to me. And I was going to read the final book in the *Dirty Tricks* series before anyone else in the world (not counting Soph and Abs, obviously)! All in all, I couldn't help but be grateful that I lived up to my nickname, Nosy Parker. Having a nose for mysteries definitely rocks!

Hollie's Hints

Wanna be a megastar writer? Find out how from superstar author, Hollie Fraser!

- Read, read, read! The best authors are all bookworms, so you're already doing one thing right!

- Create characters that you'd like to meet. That way, if your book gets made into a film, you might get to help cast some total hunks!

- Be a secret-keeper! Make sure your book is full of suspense. You don't everyone knowing the ending before they've even started reading, do you?

- Gain writing experience wherever you can! I started off at a magazine, so why not see if you can write for your school paper?

- I write all my books in a notepad. There's something satisfying about scribbling down stories on paper that you don't get with a computer.

- Be passionate! If fashion is your thing (like it is for yours truly!) then let it show in your writing. My leading ladies always wear Fabconis, just like me!

REMEMBER: STAY STYLISH!

Fact File

NAME: Hollie Fraser

AGE: 44

STAR SIGN: Aries

HAIR: Dark brown

EYES: Green

LOVES: Writing, of course! She loves nothing better than curling up with a hot choccy with tons of marshmallows and scribbling away in her notebook

HATES: Being told what to do. No one but Hollie gets to say what happens in the Dirty Tricks series!

LAST SEEN: Arriving at a casting for the new Mark Green, surrounded by brown-eyed cuties!

MOST LIKELY TO SAY: 'My fans are my biggest inspiration. Well, my fans AND my new pair of Fabconis'

WORST CRINGE EVER: When the heel of my fave Fabconis broke right before I went to one of my book launch parties and I had to borrow some stinky trainers to wear instead. Sooo not a good look with my gorge dress!

For more fact files, visit www.mega-star.co.uk

Megastar

Everyone has blushing blunders - here are some from your Megastar Mysteries friends!

Rosie

Nan got Mum and me these matching rucksacks last Christmas – yeah, I know, it's seriously uncool to match with your Mum, but there's Nan for you. Anyway, I packed up my PE kit in mine and chucked it by the front door one night. I grabbed a rucksack on the way to school the next day, but it wasn't until I started getting changed for netball that I realised I'd picked up Mum's bag of Banana Splits costumes by mistake! Even on a good day I look like a spider in a washing machine when I play netball, so just imagine what a wally I looked dressed in Mum's dodgy eighties outfit at the same time – quelle horreur!

Abs

I'd got it into my head that I was a great cook, and decided to invite Rosie and Soph over for a special tea. I read loads of recipe books and picked out some yummy-sounding cakes to make. But nothing quite went to plan, and when I finally dished out the cakes, Rosie and Soph only ate a few crumbs each! Rosie wrinkled her nose like crazy when she tried the chocolate cake – maybe it was because I spilt my glass of orange squash into the bowl while I was mixing it up. I thought chocolate and orange could be a great combo! And I think my specs must have got steamed up when I was grabbed the sugar for the cherry biscuits, cos they turned out salty, not sweet! We all had a laugh about it, but it wasn't quite the classy tea party I had planned!

Cringes

Soph

I always make the costumes for the school play, and last time Mr Lord said I could come on at the end and take a bow with all the actors. I decided to whip up an extra costume for my own moment of fame, and planned this brilliant customised top in silver and pink with matching hot-pink shorts – so cool! But just before the first performance, Mr Lord caught sight of me in it and decided that it was the perfect costume for the lead role. He made me swap clothes with Miss Perfect, Amanda Hawkins. She got to wear my amazing creation on stage while I wore the not-so-flattering number I had designed for her. Cringe!

Josh

I was getting ready for my most important scene in the latest *Dirty Tricks* movie and I didn't like the way my make-up had been done. I crept into the make-up trailer when no one was around and added a bit of extra slap to make sure I was looking my best. But as the cameras began to roll, I felt my cheeks begin to burn. Within a couple of minutes it felt like my face was on fire and I had to run off set. Whatever I'd rubbed on my face had given me an enormous rash! The director was furious as we lost a day of filming waiting for it to calm down. I don't know what made me redder, my blushes or my rash!

Hollie

I'd been looking forward to the glamorous Crystal Book Awards party for weeks, and was so excited as I slipped into a silver silk skirt, sequinned top and gorgeous matching Fabconi shoes. I couldn't believe how many A-list celebs and TV cameras were there when I arrived. When my name was called out as an award winner, I grabbed my glass of champagne, leapt to my feet and dashed to the stage. But my high heels got caught up in a stray handbag strap and I went flying through the air, knocking an enormous ice sculpture over right on top of a celeb-filled table. Shrieks filled the air and little pieces of ice rained down into my hair. I eventually arrived on stage looking red and bedraggled, only to notice that I had spilt my champagne, making a suspicious-looking wet patch on my lovely silk skirt. Oh, the shame!

What Would Your Best-selling Book Be?

Answer the questions to discover what kind of novel could make you the next Hollie Fraser!

1. How often do you write stories?

A. Only when I have to for homework

B. Every one of my schoolbooks has got a bit of a story scribbled in the back

C. Whenever I think of a good plot

D. I add to my novel every day!

2. What are you famous for at school?

A. Losing the class hamster when I looked after it for the weekend

B. Keeping the whole class in stitches with my carefully-planned pranks

C. Dressing up as a wizard on Book Day

D. Scoring the winning goals in netball

3. What would be your perfect party?

A. A trip to the zoo – I'm animal mad!

B. I love all parties – any excuse to hang out with my mates

C. I love to sparkle at a disco

D. Anything outdoors – barbeques are the best

4. What's your favourite subject at school?

A. Geography – learning about the outdoors is cool

B. Anything – school rocks!

C. Science – those chemistry experiments are magic!

D. PE – games is the best!

For more coolissimo quizzes, visit www.mega-star.co.uk

5. What is the most special thing that you own?

A. My pet
B. My photo album
C. My favourite piece of jewellery
D. Something I got on holiday

Now see what you got...

Mostly As: Animal Mad

Cute and cuddly critters are your passion, so you'd like to write a story all about animals. You might be inspired by a talking pig, a dancing penguin or a dinosaur revival, but one thing's for sure: if you write a book about animals, it will make you famous!

Mostly Bs: School Star

Hey, no one loves homework, but you actually really like school. You get to hang out with your mates, hear all the goss in the playground and chat to dreamy teachers like Mr Adams. What's not to like? So why not write a book about all the cool stuff that goes on at your school? It's bound to be a best-seller!

Mostly Cs: Miss Magic

Reading stories about extraordinary powers is your fave hobby, so why not write one of your own? Making up secret spells and magical powers sounds like heaps of fun. You might even discover that you've got a magical talent for writing once you get started. Go on – give it a try!

Mostly Ds: Awesome Adventurer

You're always dreaming about getting caught up in amazing crime-fighting storylines, so it's time to put pen to paper and write your own adventure story. And who better to play the heroine than YOU?! Maybe you'll get to play yourself in the film of your own book one day – now THAT would be cool!

Pam's Problem Page

Never fear, Pam's here to sort you out!

Dear Pam,

I've got a problem with my latest book and I just don't know what to do. I think it would be really exciting if one of the main characters died at the end, but people are putting pressure on me to keep him alive. I just want to write the best book I can, but I'm worried about what might happen to me if I don't do what these people say!

Hollie

Pam says: Hollie, my love, You've come to the right lady if you've got a problem to do with writing stories. I'm a bit of a writer myself, you see. Just give me a bell if you'd like to read my latest script, Murder on the Borehurst Express. Anyway, back to your problem. As Miss Marple would say, sometimes the answer is in the question. You've already told me what you need to do: write the best book you can. Just sit these people down with a cup of tea and a garibaldi and you'll win them round in no time. There's not much a squashed fly biscuit can't sort out, you know. Good luck with the book, young lady!

Can't wait for the next
book in the series?
Here's a sneak preview of

Ruby

Chapter One

When it comes to buying birthday presents, I am officially a genius. I've known my best friend, Abs, practically forever, but every year I come up with an even cooler present than the last one. I have this formula where you write down the person's name, the stuff they like and dislike and then the present they'd want if you were mega-rich and could buy anything. Then you add an extra bit at the bottom for a version of the present you can afford.

So, for Abs's birthday, it went like this:

Person: Abs

Likes: Me and Soph (i.e. best friends), music, shopping, make-up, TV, books, animals and chocolate

Dislikes: Amanda Hawkins, boring films, drama lessons, cabbage and Amanda Hawkins

Present she would ask for if I was mega-rich: A trip to New York

Similar thing that I can afford:
A chocolate skyscraper (not life-size, obviously) and a new lipgloss called American Sweetheart

Brilliant, eh?

Unfortunately for Abs, not everyone is quite up to my incredibly high standards on the present-buying front. Like her parents. Did they buy her the new mobile she's been dropping massivo hints about for the last month? Or a CD player to replace the one that hasn't worked since her little sis tried to feed it a biscuit? No, they did not.

'So what did you get?' me and Soph asked Abs when she arrived at school on the morning of her birthday. Checking the present-haul is always top priority on birthdays.

Abs pulled a glossy leaflet out of her bag and passed it to us. 'A day in a recording studio,' she said, sounding not-at-all-thrilled.

'You lie!' said Soph.

'I wish,' said Abs. 'Why couldn't they just have got me the phone?'

'This is so cool,' I said, reading the leaflet. 'You record any songs you want, then they turn it into a professional CD and even take your photo to go on the CD cover.'

'It'll be seriously cringe-issimo,' Abs argued. 'I can't stand there and sing in front of some record producer. I don't even sing in the shower in case Mum and Dad hear.'

'But you've got a really good voice,' said Soph, who sounds like a sackful of cheesed-off cats when she sings.

'What about when we were Mirage's backing singers?' I chipped in. The three of us had solved this huge mystery for Mirage Mullins just after her first single got to number one, and she'd thanked us by letting us be her backing singers. 'We were on stage in front of hundreds of people.'

'That was different,' said Abs. 'We were miming, remember?'

I flipped through the leaflet again, then handed it back to Abs, pointing at the second page.

'It says "Solo singers and groups welcome",' I said. 'Me and Soph could come with you.'

Abs hesitated. 'Really?'

'Course. I mean, if it makes you feel better . . .'

'Totally,' said Abs, looking much happier. 'It would be a million times easier with all of us there.'

'What are friends for?' said Soph.

Me and Abs grinned.

'In your case, Soph,' I said, 'to make everyone else sound better than Britney.'

* * *

Abs's day in the studio was booked for the following Saturday, and by the time we got there we were all majorly excited. Soph had spent the whole week turning another of her weird charity-shop finds into a seriously cool outfit for the occasion, while me and Abs had sent about a million texts trying to decide what we were going to sing. We'd narrowed it down to Fusion's latest single (in honour of the fact I met them last year and got to snog très gorge lead singer, Maff), one of the songs we'd sung on stage with Mirage last year (because it's a mega-cool memory) and Abs's favourite Girls Aloud hit (because they rock). My mum was a bit sulky when she found out we hadn't gone with any of her suggestions. As I pointed out, this is the twenty-first century and unless they had a parent in a Bananarama tribute band like I have, the producers would probably never have heard of half the eighties stuff she'd suggested.

Icon Studios was pretty cool. Considering we were in Fleetwich – the only place in the world that makes our dullsville hometown, Borehurst, look like a hive of thrill-a-minute activity – I'd half expected it to be yet another grey tower block, but it totally wasn't. Abs's mum had driven us in through a narrow passage between a bank and a shop selling fishing equipment (I told you it was exciting), into a sort of hidden courtyard. The studio building stretched around three sides in a squared-off U-shape, and was a strange mixture of old brick and shiny new glass. It looked seriously smart and showbizzy.

'I could so imagine being a huge star, turning up here in my chauffeur-driven limo,' whispered Soph as we walked through the glass doors, which had slid open silently to let us through.

'D'you know where we're meant to go?' I asked Abs, looking round at the super-sleek reception area. The walls were lined with CD-cover artwork in silver frames and there was a curving metal and wooden staircase in the corner.

'Reception,' said Abs, walking over to the huge, white reception desk.

A few seconds later, she came back.

'The receptionist says to take a seat and our producer will be out in a minute.'

The three of us perched on a row of cool orange chairs set against one wall. The receptionist gave us a faint smile. There was a corridor opposite us with a sign that said 'Studios A-E'. As I watched, a tall, brown-haired dream-god walked along it towards us.

'Abigail?' he said.

'Hi,' I said swoonily.

'Er, *I'm* Abigail,' said Abs, flashing me one of her famous death-stares.

'Will,' said Mr Dreamy, shaking her hand. 'I'm your producer.'

'These are my friends,' said Abs. 'Soph,' – Soph shook his hand – 'and –'

'Posie,' I interrupted, sticking my hand out. 'Posie Rarker. I mean Rarky Poser.'

'Rosie Parker,' Abs corrected me.

'It's good to meet you all,' said Will.

He gave me a bit of a funny look, and I realised I was still shaking his hand. I let go, and smiled at him in what I hoped was a reassuringly I-am-not-a-mad-person way.

'Shall we make a start?' he said, backing away from me quite quickly.

Rosie Parker's really useful guide to recording your own CD:

1. Listen very carefully when your dream-god producer is giving you a tour of the studio. The room where you sing into the microphone is called the live room, not the padded room. Padded rooms are only found in loony bins.

2. The producer's bit of the studio is the control room. The giant desk with all the knobs and buttons and slidey bits is the mixing desk. If you ask 'what does that one do?' about every single one, you will end up with less than half an hour to actually sing your songs and will still not really understand the knobs.

3. Leaning in to the microphone and saying 'one-two, one-two, testing, one-two' will not make anyone except you laugh.

4. Just because you cannot hear your producer through the glass window in the live room, it is not safe to assume he cannot hear you. Going on about how gorgey he is, then watching him look horrified is not a good way of testing who can hear who.

5. When your producer suggests you should warm up, he means warm up your voice by singing through your songs a few times, not warm up your body by doing star jumps and jogging on the spot.

6. Trying to flip your hair (as recommended in *Star Secrets'* Twenty Top Flirting Tips feature) when you're wearing headphones is not a) safe, b) a good idea, or c) at all attractive.

7. Saying 'cheese' when having your photo taken for the CD cover will make your smile look like Wallace from *Wallace and Gromit*. (Do I need to explain why this is not a good thing?)

8. Getting really into the song and deciding to try some Christina-Aguilera-style improvisation

will just make the producer think you've forgotten the tune. Don't add in extra 'oh yeah' or 'ooh, baby' bits, either.

'That's great,' said Will as we finished the last song.

'Are you sure?' said Abs. 'Soph was squawking in the last chorus.'

'Oi!' said Soph indignantly. 'I do *not* squawk. The microphone must have been out of tune.'

Will grinned. 'Take off your headphones, come in here and let's have a listen.'

He pulled three extra chairs up to his mixing desk for us.

'This,' he said, 'is the good bit.'

'I thought our singing was the good bit,' I said.

'Yeees,' he said slowly, looking a bit shiftily in Soph's direction. 'But this . . . helps things along – smoothes everything out. Listen.'

He pressed a couple of buttons and the room was suddenly filled with the sound of our voices over the backing track. Me and Abs gaped at each other, horrified. It sounded très terrible.

'Cool,' said Soph, nodding her head along to the music.

She really is completely tone deaf.

Will turned it down a bit.

'If I do this,' he said, fiddling on the desk again, 'I can separate your voices out. So that's just Rosie.'

We listened for a minute. Sometimes I wonder if it's fair to deprive the world of my marvelloso voice by being a mega-successful journalist instead of a singer.

'This is Abs,' said Will, switching to a different voice and forgetting to comment on my brilliantness. 'And then Soph.'

Which was where it sort of fell apart.

'Is there a dog loose in the studio?' said Abs, and Soph kicked her in the shins.

Will laughed and tapped away at the computer which was sitting next to his mixing desk, then pressed play again.

'Who's that?' I said, as a fourth voice filled the studio.

'Soph,' he said.

'No way!' me and Abs said together.

'Oh, yeah,' said Soph. 'I totally rock.'

'How did you do that?' I asked.

'It's called pitch correction,' Will explained. 'It turns all Soph's wrong notes into the right ones so she's in tune.'

'We should get one of those for the music room at school,' said Abs, as Will carried on working.

'Maybe we could have one fitted in Soph's hairbrush,' I suggested.

* * *

Twenty minutes later, Will had finished pitch-correcting Soph, and worked a few more producery tricks on our songs. We now sounded like a serious threat to the Sugababes. We'd chosen a photo for the CD cover from the ones he'd taken earlier, and even though I was trying really hard to get some gossip from Will about celebs he had worked with, we'd just about run out of excuses to hang around.

'It's my mum,' said Abs, opening the text message she'd just received. 'She's waiting outside.'

We all said thanks to Will, and he reminded us to order extra copies of our CD in reception before we left.

'You did a great job,' he said.

'I still can't believe that was my voice,' said Soph as we walked back along the studio corridor.

'Me neither,' said Abs.

'Will thought we were great,' I said dreamily.

'Maybe we should start a group,' said Abs.

'Oui, oui!' Soph flung her arms out towards an invisible audience. 'Ladies and gentlemen, live from boring Borehurst, please welcome Soph and the Sophettes!'

'Hey,' I said, 'since when was this *your* band?'

'Yeah,' said Abs, with an evil glint in her eye. 'How about "Please welcome the Rarky Posers" instead?'

I felt my face turn redder than a monkey's bum. 'I couldn't help it. It's not my fault he's –'

But before I could say anything else, we crashed

into this complete stranger who'd appeared out of nowhere. As soon as we'd untangled ourselves, I realised she'd just come out of one of the other studios along the corridor.

'I'm really sorry,' I said to the stranger, who didn't look that much older than us. 'We totally weren't watching where we were going.'

'Are you OK?' Soph asked.

'I'm fine,' she grinned.

'We should've been paying more attention,' said Abs. 'We were just messing about.'

'I heard,' said the girl, still smiling. 'So who's Rarky Poser?'

I blushed again. 'That'd be me,' I said. 'Rosie Parker.'

'Nice to meet you, Rosie Parker,' she said. 'I'm Ruby Munday.'

I stared at her, wondering why that name sounded familiar.

'Awful, isn't it?' she nodded. 'I probably should have changed it.'

'How d'you mean, awful?' said Soph.

'Ruby Munday. Like the song, "Ruby Tuesday",' said Ruby.

'The Rolling Stones!' said Abs. 'My dad loves them.'

Ruby nodded. 'My parents have been fans for years. When I was born, they thought it would be really hilarious to call me Ruby, and I've been stuck with people making jokes about it ever since.'

'Sounds like they'd get on with my mum,' I said grimly. 'I mean, who in their right mind calls their daughter Rosie when their surname is Parker?'

Ruby laughed. 'So are you three in a band, then?' she said.

'I wish,' said Soph.

Abs explained about her birthday present. 'We've had a brilliant time. This place is awesome.'

'It's OK, isn't it?' Ruby agreed. 'I'm here loads at the moment.'

'Are you in a band?' asked Abs.

'No,' said Ruby. 'I'm recording an album, but it's just me. I mean, I've got backing musicians, but

I write my own songs, and sing, and play a bit of guitar and stuff.'

'That must be so cool,' I said.

She frowned, and I noticed how tired she looked. 'I love it, but it's my first album and it has to be perfect, you know? There's a lot of pressure to get it just right, or I might not get the chance to make another.' She smiled again. 'It *is* a pretty cool job most of the time, though.'

The studio door opened and a man wearing a black hat stuck his head out. 'We need you back in fifteen, Rubes,' he told her.

Ruby pointed at another door a little way along the corridor. According to a paper sign taped to it, it was the chill-out lounge. 'I really need to go and get some coffee,' she said. 'And, you know . . .'

'Chill out?' said Abs.

'Exactly,' Ruby giggled. 'It was really good to meet you all.'

'You, too,' I said.

Abs looked at her watch. 'My mum is going to kill us,' she said.